Agatha Christie

MARK CAMPBELL

POCKET ESSENTIALS

This edition published in 2015
by Pocket Essentials,
an imprint of Oldcastle Books Ltd,
PO Box 394, Harpenden,
Herts, AL5 1XJ

www.pocketessentials.com

A CIP catalogue record for this book is available from the British Library.

ISBN
978-1-84344-423-7 (print)
978-1-84344-424-4 (epub)
978-1-84344-425-1 (kindle)
978-1-84344-426-8 (pdf)

4 6 8 10 9 7 5

Typeset in Univers Light with Myriad Pro display
by Avocet Typeset, Somerton, Somerset, TA11 6RT
Printed in Great Britain by Clays Ltd, St Ives plc

For Mum and Gran

Acknowledgements

I am indebted to the following people who have helped me get this book finished: to the person I can't name for help above and beyond the call of duty, to Andy Slater for donating his PC to a very worthy cause (me), to Mary for proofreading, emotional support and generally keeping the children out of my hair, to the Slade Library staff for their usual friendliness and to the staff of the BFI, the NFT, the British Museum and Madame Tussaud's – to each and every one, I extend a heartfelt thank you. My thanks also to David Wilkins, Julia Beaver, Nancy Lee Child and John Curran for supplying further information.

Contents

Foreword by Simon Brett

Some contemporary crime writers are a bit sniffy about Agatha Christie, but I've always been a great admirer. As an author, she achieved what she set out to do, and was more massively successful than she could ever have anticipated.

To complain that she didn't write slice-of-life realist novels seems to me as misguided as to criticise Shakespeare for not writing any operas. That was not what he was trying to do. Agatha Christie had a comparable knowledge of her skills and limitations. She aimed to write literate, entertaining crime novels that would puzzle and confuse – but never cheat – her readers. And that's what she achieved – magnificently.

She also helped to define the crime novel. Though nobody now writes the same sort of books except as pastiche, Agatha Christie still casts a long shadow over the genre. Taking her cue from that other great shadow-caster, Conan Doyle's Sherlock Holmes, she developed the amateur detective into the dandified, infuriating but brilliant Hercule Poirot. She also created the archetypal observant little-old-lady sleuth in Miss Marple, and she set them both in a world where the only rôle of the official police force was to be permanently baffled. Agatha Christie's characters have spawned many descendants in crime fiction over the years.

Her other huge skill lay in her plotting. Until examining her books, it is hard to imagine that so many legitimate ways exist for an author to fool readers. One of the reasons why nobody now writes the sort of puzzle novel that Agatha Christie made her own is that she thought of and developed all the best puzzles. There aren't any left.

And now lovers of Agatha Christie's work – or those unaware of its breadth and scope – can have all the important details to hand in this neatly-packaged little volume by Mark Campbell. I'll certainly always have a copy handy.

Simon Brett
August 2001

Simon Brett worked as a light entertainment producer in radio and television before taking up writing full time in 1979. Since then he has written over sixty books, more than half of them crime novels, including *Situation Tragedy* (1981), *Mrs, Presumed Dead* (1988) and *Death on the Downs* (2001); his 1984 novel *A Shock to the System* was made into a film starring Michael Caine. He is also the author of the radio and television series *After Henry* and the bestselling book *How to be a Little Sod*. A former Chairman of the Crime Writers' Association and the Society of Authors, Brett is President of the Detection Club and lives in an Agatha Christie-style village on the South Downs.

1

The Puppet-Master

It was the covers that did it for me. I would peruse the crime shelves of our local Bournemouth bookshops – a scrawny ten-year-old with unruly blonde hair and National Health glasses – and drink deeply of those violent, nightmarish images: telephones dripping with blood, skulls grinning out of golf balls, eyeballs poking from blood-spattered tennis racquets... it's a wonder I wasn't scarred for life. (Actually, that's a moot point.) And each time I'd slide a book from the shelf, the name 'Agatha Christie' in big, bold letters would stare back at me (like that dratted eyeball). Yes, she – and Dick Francis, ugh, his covers were terrifying too – would guarantee a brief spine-chilling thrill in the bustling first floor of WH Smith, when I was probably supposed to be looking for Enid Blyton.

Then a few years later I read one. It was *Murder on the Orient Express*. Well, all I can say is I've never seen such a flagrant flaunting of the Trade Descriptions Act. Where was the dripping blood? The gouged eyeballs? The grinning skull on a mound of worm-infested earth? They were nowhere to be seen. All I got was a posh train, a load of upper-class people speaking in old-fashioned language, and a very confusing story about one person after another being accused of killing someone (in a very bloodless way, I was disappointed to find). The covers may have promised blood and guts (those '70s cover artists – what were they on?), but the contents couldn't be more different – they were as gentle and dated as a pat on the shoulder from your great-aunt.

So I didn't read many more after that. (After a brief love affair with the Pan Books of Horror Stories, I turned to James Herbert and the odd Stephen King. Gouged eyeballs aplenty there.) But of course the thing I'd missed – the thing that those covers claimed in spades – was that these light, genteel murder mysteries were far more gripping precisely *because* they were so bloodless. Death stalked in broad daylight down some country lane, a person everyone hated would end up murdered in a conspicuous location, all the villagers would be suspected... it wasn't the blood that was scary, it was the paranoia. And you can't paint paranoia on a book cover.

As a child, the idea of paranoia was too abstract to get my head round – it's an adult fear really and, thankfully, most of the time it has no basis in reality (except, of course, for us writers). But it happens all the time with Agatha Christie. Pick up one of her books and you will have absolutely no idea whodunit – it could be anyone. And I mean *anyone*. And there's nothing cosy about that, is there? We need reassurance, we need to tell the goodies from the baddies. It's a strange and rather terrifying notion when we can't, and Christie delights in denying us this privilege. She will choose who's guilty, she will deceive with her bluff and double-bluff, she will show you just who's in charge. And you, the reader, stumble blindly in her shadow.

Paranoia goes hand-in-hand with claustrophobia, and thus Christie's best stories are ones that make a feature of small settings and small casts. Her globetrotting thrillers automatically disappoint by moving around so much – we need to feel isolated, trapped; be it in a hotel on a desolate island or the book-lined study of a smart country house snowed up for the winter. Christie is an absolute genius at using similar ingredients over and over, and yet each time providing new thrills, new twists, new rushes of anticipation and horror. Even the worst of her books has its own unique *frisson* of excitement. She just can't help it – even in her eighties, she still came up with the goods.

Her critics say she wrote glorified crossword puzzles – meticulously plotted narratives that turned her characters into zombiefied ciphers who had to be in place 'A' by point 'B' in order to overhear person 'C'. Well, yes, there is an element of that. But within these contrivances, there is a huge amount of 'give'. Her characters exhibit real personalities, their motivations are for the most part believable, and the interplay between them is always a joy. For Christie's observance of the nuances of conversation is second to none. She captures the curious half-sentences and ungrammatical constructions that we call 'talking' and slaps them straight down onto the page. It's like we're hearing *real* conversation, and of course that's where she wrong-foots us – within these throwaway lines are clues that *she* has planted, not the characters. Remember, she is the puppet-master, even when her creations seem to have a life of their own.

People mainly read Agatha Christie for one reason – a book written by her is a guarantee of a good story, reasonably well told, with a hard-to-guess ending. There's nothing too deep in her books (although she is, accidentally, a social historian of some note), but what there is is set down with such a casual air of authority that you feel obliged to pay attention. Her lowbrow reputation masks her highbrow techniques – she is one of this country's finest novelists (crime or otherwise) – if you haven't done so already, go out and buy, borrow or steal *The Murder of Roger Ackroyd* and you'll see I'm right.

Those 1970s covers might have been scary, but the stuff inside is a whole lot scarier.

2

Dame Agatha Christie Biography

"If anybody writes about my life in the future, I'd rather they got the facts right."

Agatha Christie, quoted in *The Sunday Times,* 27 February 1966.

Agatha Mary Clarissa Miller was born at her parents' home of Ashfield in Barton Road, Tor Mohun, a district of Torquay, on 15 September 1890. She was the last of Frederick and Clarissa Miller's three children: Margaret ('Madge') Frary was born in 1879, and Louis ('Monty') Montant arrived a year later. Educated at home, she taught herself to read and write at an early age – her first published piece was a poem about electric trams printed in an Ealing newspaper when she was 11, the same year that her father died of pneumonia. In 1910, after Christie's return from a Parisian finishing school, she and her mother spent the winter months in Egypt, an experience that would stay with her for the rest of her life.

Back in England she had some of her poetry published in *The Poetry Review* and won some prizes. But her attempts at stories were less successful: writing under the pen names of 'Mac Miller' and 'Nathaniel Miller' they were rejected. Her mother suggested that local author Eden Philpotts might be permitted to give her some advice. He proved very encouraging, complimenting her on her grasp of structure and dialogue and recommending that she continue writing.

She became engaged in 1912 to Major Reggie Lucy, but while he was serving in Hong Kong she fell in love with Lt Archibald Christie of the Royal Field Artillery. They married 18 months later on Christmas Eve 1914, with Archie now a Captain in the Royal Flying Corps. He went to war two days later, and Christie began working as a nurse in Torbay Hospital, later moving to the dispensary where she acquired her knowledge of poisons. Remembering her sister's claim years before that she couldn't write a detective story, she decided to prove her wrong and began working on one during quiet periods at the dispensary. Poison would be central to the plot of *The Mysterious Affair at Styles*, her first published novel (and the *Pharmaceutical Journal* would later write approvingly of her knowledge).

Archie, now a Colonel, was posted to the London Air Ministry in 1918. They moved into two rooms on the second floor of 5 Northwick Terrace in St John's Wood, London, now demolished. After the birth of her only child Rosalind Margaret Clarissa on 5 August 1919, they needed a larger flat, so moved into first 25 and then 96 Addison Mansions, an apartment block behind Olympia in Earls Court. In 1922 the Christies travelled round the world with Archie's friend, Major Belcher, organiser of the British Empire Exhibition Mission: they visited South Africa, Australia, New Zealand, stopped off for a brief holiday in Honolulu, and finally ended up in Canada. On their return in December, Archie got a job at the city firm of Austral Trust Ltd and they moved into a house called Scotswood in Sunningdale, about thirty miles from central London. In 1924 they moved to a larger house in the same area which they nicknamed Styles, in honour of Christie's first book.

Christie's mother died of bronchitis in 1926, and shortly afterwards Archie revealed that he had fallen in love with another woman – Nancy Neele, a joint acquaintance – and wanted a divorce. On 3 December, after a quarrel, Archie left Styles to spend the weekend with Ms Neele in Godalming, Surrey. That evening Christie left the house, leaving her daughter asleep, and left a letter for her secretary saying that she was going to Yorkshire. She posted another to the Deputy Chief Constable for Surrey, saying she feared for her life. Next day her car was found by a gypsy, abandoned by the side of the road at Newlands Corner, near Guildford in Surrey. But Christie was nowhere to be found. The *Daily News* offered £100 for information leading to her whereabouts, a pool near the car was dredged, and police from Surrey, Essex, Berkshire and Kent were drafted in to look for her. Archie Christie was the chief suspect, and many false trails were followed up. A week after her disappearance, 15,000 volunteers searched the Merrow Downs where her car had been found, but discovered nothing. Thriller writer Edgar Wallace postulated in the *Daily Mail* that she had faked her disappearance to spite her husband and that she was probably alive and well in London.

Wallace was partially right. A banjo player at the Hydropathic Hotel in Harrogate – now the Old Swan Hotel – had been thinking for a few days that one of the guests could have been the missing novelist. He told the Harrogate police and shortly afterwards the news was leaked to the press. The *Daily Mail* sent a special train filled with reporters and photographers, and reporter Ritchie Calder accosted her directly. The game was up – Christie admitted who she was, and on Tuesday 14 December the London *Evening Standard* reported that the hunt was over.

Christie had booked into the hotel on 4 December as 'Mrs Theresa Neele' from Cape Town. She had spent the time there like any other guest, taking tea in a local tea shop, going on walks and playing billiards; she had even posted an announcement in *The Times* asking for friends and relatives to contact 'Neele' at a particular box number. Archie came up to the Hydro on the 14th and identified her and two doctors issued a statement claiming she had suffered a loss of memory. Various theories have sprung up since then – some claim she had planned the whole thing, others that it was a publicity stunt to sell her latest book – but from then on, one thing became clear: she hated publicity, and spent the rest of her life actively shunning it.

A divorce was granted in April 1928 and Archie then married Nancy Neele, who died of cancer in 1958, Archie dying four years later. In 1929 Christie bought a mews house in Chelsea: 22 Creswell Place. She met the archaeologist Max Mallowan in 1930 while he was conducting a dig at Arpachiyah in Iraq; they fell in love and married in Scotland in September of that year, shortly after the publication of her first romantic novel, written under the pseudonym of Mary Westmacott.

From then on, the couple divided their time between England and the Middle East. Further houses were purchased: 48 Sheffield Terrace in Kensington, London, and Winterbrook House in Wallingford, Oxon. They even built their own house at Chagar Bazar in Syria where Christie began a diary that formed the basis of her memoir *Come, Tell Me How You Live*. In autumn 1936 the expedition dug up seventy cuneiform tablets which linked Chagar Bazar with the Royal House of Assyria – a significant historical find.

In 1938 the Christies bought another property – a large Georgian house overlooking the river Dart near Galmpton, a few miles upriver from Torquay. This was Greenway House, and they would live here, on and off, for the rest of their lives. During the Second World War, the property became a nursery for London-evacuated children and later accommodation for United States Navy personnel. For a while Christie returned to her job at the Torbay Hospital dispensary before joining Max in London, where he had a job at the Air Ministry. They lived in a succession of flats: Half Moon Street, Park Place, then Sheffield Terrace. When this last place was bombed, they moved to a modern block of flats at 22 Lawn Road, Hampstead. Christie worked as a dispenser at University College Hospital, while Max was seconded to

North Africa, where he became an adviser on Arab affairs. Away from Max, she spent much of her free time writing.

In 1943 Christie's daughter Rosalind married Hubert Prichard, a soldier in the Royal Welch Fusiliers, and on 21 September she gave birth to Mathew. Tragically Hubert was killed in action a year later, and Rosalind married again in 1949, to barrister and oriental scholar Anthony Hicks. In the same year Christie accompanied Mallowan (by air, what she called a "dull routine") for the most important archaeological dig of his career – to Nimrud, the ancient military capital of Assyria. They would return there every year for almost a decade. In 1954 Christie's secondary career as a playwright reached its acme, with three shows running concurrently in London: *The Mousetrap*, *Witness for the Prosecution* and *Spider's Web*.

In 1950 she was made a Fellow of the Royal Society of Literature, and on 1 January 1956 she became a Commander of the British Empire. Max received the same honour four years later. Crippling taxation forced the author to set up a private company, Agatha Christie Ltd; in 1968 Bookers Books, a subsidiary of agricultural and industrial conglomerate Booker McConnell bought a 51% stake, increasing later to 64%. The remainder was held by Christie's daughter and grandson. In June 1998 Booker sold their shares to international media company Chorion Ltd. In 2012, following a management buyout, they in turn sold their 64% stake to Acorn Media UK, a subsidiary of RLJ Entertainment Inc.

A 1959 UNESCO report claimed that Christie had been translated into 103 languages – with sales of around 400 million copies to date, she came third after the Bible and Shakespeare. Mallowan was knighted in 1968, and three years later, aged 81, Christie was made Dame Commander of the British Empire. On 16 June that year she broke her leg in a fall at her home in Wallingford and this led to a decline in her health; for the rest of her life she walked with a stick and made few public appearances. In March 1972 she was measured for Madame Tussaud's Wax Museum and shortly afterwards her life-size figure appeared in the conservatory, seated below film director Alfred Hitchcock. She still resides there to this day – seated now in the Grand Hall.

A banquet at Claridge's, after the London gala premiere of *Murder on the Orient Express* in November 1974, was the last public event Christie attended. Interviewed by Lord Snowdon for the *Toronto Star* of 14 December 1974, she was asked what she wanted to be remembered for. "Well, I would like it to be said that I was a good writer of detective and thriller stories," she replied. *Curtain*, written during the Second World War, was published in 1975. A few days into the following year, just after luncheon on 12 January, she died at Winterbrook after a short cold. She was buried four days later following a private service in St Mary's Church in the nearby village of Cholsey. The tombstone inscription, a quotation from Edmund Spenser's *The Faerie Queene*, reads:

"Sleepe after toyle, port after stormie seas,
Ease after war, death after life, does greatly please."

3

Complete Checklist of Agatha Christie's Works

78 books, 157 short stories

Books

Where the titles were published in Britain and America, the American editions appeared either in the same year or the year after (very occasionally the year before): except where the difference is significant, only the UK publication date is given. For books that appeared in only one of these countries, the following symbols apply: † = UK, * = US. (These symbols are used throughout the book.) Original titles are quoted in this list, with 'and other stories' (where relevant) usually removed in later printings and, for brevity's sake, elsewhere in this guide. Anthologies (by various authors) and collected works are excluded.

Each book is examined in more detail later in this guide. For example, POIROT 1 is the first book in the Poirot section

ACM = Agatha Christie Mallowan
MW = Mary Westmacott
ss = short stories

1. *The Mysterious Affair at Styles* (1920) – POIROT 1
2. *The Secret Adversary* (1922) – TOMMY & TUPPENCE 1
3. *Murder on the Links* (aka *The Murder on the Links*) (1923) – POIROT 2
4. *Poirot Investigates* (1924, ss) – POIROT 3
5. *The Man in the Brown Suit* (1924) – THRILLER 1
6. *The Road of Dreams* (1924) – POEMS 1
7. *The Secret of Chimneys* (1925) – THRILLER 2
8. *The Murder of Roger Ackroyd* (1926) – POIROT 4
9. *The Big Four* (1927) – POIROT 5
10. *The Mystery of the Blue Train* (1928) – POIROT 6
11. *The Seven Dials Mystery* (1929) – THRILLER 3

12. *Partners in Crime* (1929, ss) – TOMMY & TUPPENCE 2
13. *The Mysterious Mr Quin* (1930, ss) – QUIN 1
14. *The Murder at the Vicarage* (1930) – MARPLE 1
15. *Giant's Bread* (1930) – ROMANCE 1 (MW)
16. *The Sittaford Mystery* / US: *The Murder at Hazelmoor* (1931) – MYSTERY 1
17. *The Floating Admiral* (1931) – COLLABORATIVE MYSTERY 1
18. *Peril at End House* (1932) – POIROT 7
19. *The Thirteen Problems* / US: *The Tuesday Club Murders* (1932, ss) – MARPLE 2
20. *Lord Edgware Dies* / US: *Thirteen at Dinner* (1933) – POIROT 8
21. *The Hound of Death and Other Stories* (1933†, ss) – MYSTERY 2 / SUPERNATURAL 1
22. *Murder on the Orient Express* / US: *Murder in the Calais Coach* (1934) – POIROT 9
23. *The Listerdale Mystery* (1934†, ss) – MYSTERY 3
24. *Why Didn't They Ask Evans?* / US: *The Boomerang Clue* (1934) – MYSTERY 4
25. *Parker Pyne Investigates* / US: *Mr Parker Pyne, Detective* (1934) – PYNE 1
26. *Unfinished Portrait* (1934) – ROMANCE 2 (MW)
27. *Three Act Tragedy* / US: *Murder in Three Acts* (1935) – POIROT 10
28. *Death in the Clouds* / US: *Death in the Air* (1935) – POIROT 11
29. *The ABC Murders* (1936) – POIROT 12
30. *Murder in Mesopotamia* (1936) – POIROT 13
31. *Cards on the Table* (1936) – POIROT 14
32. *Murder in the Mews* / US: *Dead Man's Mirror* (1937, ss) – POIROT 15
33. *Dumb Witness* / US: *Poirot Loses a Client* (aka *Mystery at Littlegreen House* and *Murder at Littlegreen House*) (1937) – POIROT 16
34. *Death on the Nile* (1937) – POIROT 17
35. *Appointment with Death* (1938) – POIROT 18
36. *Hercule Poirot's Christmas* / US: *Murder for Christmas* (aka *A Holiday for Murder*) (1938) – POIROT 19
37. *Murder is Easy* / US: *Easy to Kill* (1939) – MYSTERY 5
38. *The Regatta Mystery* (1939*, ss) – POIROT 20, MARPLE 3, SUPERNATURAL 2 & PYNE 2
39. *Ten Little Niggers* (aka *And Then There Were None*) / US: *And Then There Were None* (aka *Ten Little Indians* and *The Nursery Rhyme Murders* [1939]) – MYSTERY 6
40. *Sad Cypress* (1940) – POIROT 21
41. *One, Two, Buckle My Shoe* / US: *The Patriotic Murders* (aka *An*

Overdose of Death) (1940) – POIROT 22

42. *Evil Under the Sun* (1941) – POIROT 23
43. *N or M?* (1941) – TOMMY & TUPPENCE 3
44. *The Body in the Library* (1942) – MARPLE 4
45. *Five Little Pigs* / US: *Murder in Retrospect* (1943) – POIROT 24
46. *The Moving Finger* (1943) – MARPLE 5
47. *Towards Zero* / US: aka *Come and Be Hanged* (1944) – MYSTERY 7
48. *Absent in the Spring* (1944) – ROMANCE 3 (MW)
49. *Death Comes as the End* (1945) – MYSTERY 8
50. *Sparkling Cyanide* / US: *Remembered Death* (1945) – MYSTERY 9
51. *Poirot Knows the Murderer* (1946, ss) – POIROT 25
52. *Poirot Lends a Hand* (1946, ss) – POIROT 26 & PYNE 3
53. *Come, Tell Me How You Live* (1946) – MEMOIR 1
54. *The Hollow* / US: *Murder After Hours* (1946) – POIROT 27
55. *The Labours of Hercules* / US: *The Labors of Hercules* (1947, ss) – POIROT 28
56. *The Rose and the Yew Tree* (1948) – ROMANCE 4 (MW)
57. *Taken at the Flood* / US: *There is a Tide* (1948) – POIROT 29
58. *The Witness for the Prosecution* (aka *Witness for the Prosecution*) (1948*, ss) – POIROT 30, MYSTERY 10 & SUPERNATURAL 3
59. *Crooked House* (1949) – MYSTERY 11
60. *Three Blind Mice and Other Stories* (aka *The Mousetrap and Other Stories*) (1950*, ss) – POIROT 31, MARPLE 6, QUIN 2 & MYSTERY 12
61. *A Murder is Announced* (1950) – MARPLE 7
62. *They Came to Baghdad* (1951) – THRILLER 4
63. *The Under Dog and Other Stories* (1951*, ss) – POIROT 32
64. *Mrs McGinty's Dead* / US: aka *Blood Will Tell* (1952) – POIROT 33
65. *They Do It With Mirrors* / US: *Murder With Mirrors* (1952) – MARPLE 8
66. *A Daughter's a Daughter* (1952) – ROMANCE 5 (MW)
67. *After the Funeral* / US: *Funerals are Fatal* (1953) – POIROT 34
68. *A Pocket Full of Rye* (1953) – MARPLE 9
69. *Destination Unknown* / US: *So Many Steps to Death* (1954) – THRILLER 5
70. *Hickory Dickory Dock* / US: *Hickory Dickory Death* (1955) – POIROT 35
71. *Dead Man's Folly* (1956) – POIROT 36
72. *The Burden* (1956) – ROMANCE 6 (MW)
73. *4.50 from Paddington* / US: *What Mrs McGillicuddy Saw!* (1957) – MARPLE 10

74. *Ordeal by Innocence* (1958) – MYSTERY 13
75. *Cat Among the Pigeons* (1959) – POIROT 37
76. *The Adventure of the Christmas Pudding and a Selection of Entrées* (1960†, ss) – POIROT 38 MARPLE 11
77. *Double Sin and Other Stories* (1961*, ss) – POIROT 39, MARPLE 12 & SUPERNATURAL 4
78. *Thirteen for Luck!* (US: 1961, UK: 1966, ss) – POIROT 40 & MARPLE 13
79. *The Pale Horse* (1961) – SUPERNATURAL 5
80. *The Mirror Crack'd from Side to Side* / US: *The Mirror Crack'd* (1962) – MARPLE 14
81. *The Clocks* (1963) – POIROT 41
82. *A Caribbean Mystery* (1964) – MARPLE 15
83. *Surprise! Surprise!* (1965*, ss) – MYSTERY 14
84. *At Bertram's Hotel* (1965) – MARPLE 16
85. *Star Over Bethlehem and Other Stories* (1965) – POEMS 2 (ACM)
86. *Thirteen Clues for Miss Marple* (1966*, ss) – MARPLE 17
87. *Third Girl* (1966) – POIROT 42
88. *Endless Night* (1967) – THRILLER 5
89. *By the Pricking of My Thumbs* (1968) – TOMMY & TUPPENCE 4
90. *Hallowe'en Party* (1969) – POIROT 43
91. *Passenger to Frankfurt* (1970) – THRILLER 6
92. *The Golden Ball and Other Stories* (1971*, ss) – ROMANCE 7, MYSTERY 15 & SUPERNATURAL 6
93. *Nemesis* (1971) – MARPLE 18
94. *Elephants Can Remember* (1972) – POIROT 44
95. *Poems* (1973) – POEMS 3
96. *Postern of Fate* (1973) – TOMMY & TUPPENCE 5
97. *Poirot's Early Cases* / US: *Hercule Poirot's Early Cases* (1974, ss) – POIROT 45
98. *Curtain: Poirot's Last Case* / US: *Curtain* (1975) – POIROT 46
99. *Sleeping Murder* (1976) – MARPLE 19
100. *An Autobiography* (1977) – MEMOIRS 2
101. *Miss Marple's Final Cases and Two Other Stories* (1979†, ss) – MARPLE 20
102. *The Scoop and Behind the Screen* (1983) – COLLABORATIVE MYSTERY 2
103. *Problem at Pollensa Bay and Other Stories* (1991†, ss) – POIROT 47, PYNE 4, QUIN 3 & ROMANCE 8
104. *While the Light Lasts* (1997†, ss) – SUPERNATURAL 7, MYSTERY 15, ROMANCE 8 & POIROT 48
105. *The Harlequin Tea Set* (1997*, ss) – SUPERNATURAL 8, MYSTERY

106. *Hercule Poirot and the Greenshore Folly* (2014) – POIROT 36
     [original novella]

Stage Plays

1. *Black Coffee* (1930)
2. *Akhnaton* (unperformed, c1937)
3. *Ten Little Niggers / US: Ten Little Indians* (1943)
4. *Appointment with Death* (1945)
5. *Murder on the Nile / US: Hidden Horizon* (1946)
6. *The Hollow* (1951)
7. *The Mousetrap* (1952)
8. *Witness for the Prosecution* (1953)
9. *Spider's Web* (1954)
10. *A Daughter's a Daughter* (1956)
11. *Towards Zero* (co-written with Gerald Verner, 1956)
12. *Verdict* (1958)
13. *The Unexpected Guest* (1958)
14. *Go Back for Murder* (1960)
15. *Rule of Three* (1962)
16. *Fiddlers Three* (a revised version of *Fiddlers Five*, 1972)
17. *Chimneys* (a revised version of *The Secret of Chimneys*, 2003)

Radio and Television Plays

1. *Wasp's Nest* (1937)
2. *Yellow Iris* (1937)
3. *Three Blind Mice* (1947)
4. *Butter in a Lordly Dish* (1948)
5. *Personal Call* (1954)

4

M Hercule Poirot

33 novels, 53 short stories

Hercule Poirot

Poirot, now retired, was one of the most celebrated members of the Belgian police force. He worked with Inspector Japp on the Abercrombie forgery case of 1904 and was still active in Ostend in 1909 (*Murder on the Links*, 1923). We first encounter him in his late sixties (*The Mysterious Affair at Styles*, 1920) in the village of Styles St Mary, together with a number of other Belgian refugees. He investigates the death of Mrs Inglethorp because she extended hospitality to several of his countrymen.

He is described thus: "He was hardly more than five feet, four inches, but carried himself with great dignity. His head was exactly the shape of an egg, and he always perched it a little on one side. His moustache was very stiff and military. The neatness of his attire was almost incredible; I believe a speck of dust would have caused him more pain than a bullet wound." When first seen, he is said to limp badly, but only a little time later when inspecting Mrs Inglethorp's room, he darts around "with the agility of a grasshopper". But his appearance can be deceptive. "His faultless evening clothes, the exquisite set of his white tie, the exact symmetry of his hair parting, the sheen of pomade on his hair, and the tortured splendour of his famous moustaches – all combined to paint the perfect picture of an inveterate dandy. It was hard, at these moments, to take the little man seriously." ('The Mystery of the Baghdad Chest' – *The Regatta Mystery*, 1939*.)

He later moves to the village of King's Abbot (*The Murder of Roger Ackroyd*, 1926), but obviously seeks a faster pace of life because we soon find him residing at Whitehaven Mansions, W1 (*The ABC Murders*, 1936), an apartment block he admires for its "most pleasing symmetry". (He is obsessed with order – on one occasion he deplores the fact that hens lay eggs of different sizes.) The name of these apartments changes twice: to Whitehouse Mansions (*Cat Among the Pigeons*, 1959), then Whitefriars Mansions (*Elephants Can Remember*, 1972). His telephone number is TRA(falgar) 8137 (*Dead Man's Folly*, 1956). He sometimes escapes to the country for a weekend in a rented cottage (*The Hollow*, 1946).

He sanctifies mother-love, but is cynical about romantic attachments: "Woman are never kind, though they can sometimes be tender," he states (*After the Funeral*, 1953). The one exception is flamboyant Russian beauty Vera Rossakoff (*The Big Four*, 1927) – she is often in his thoughts, and he can't help but unfavourably compare London girls with her (*One, Two, Buckle My Shoe*, 1940). He seems generally uninterested in sex, but can be moved by great beauty, be it male or female – in *Hallowe'en Party* (1969) he observes a young man "of an unusual beauty...[he] was tall, slender, with features of great perfection such as a classical sculptor might have produced."

His chief characteristic is egotism: "I admit freely and without hypocrisy that I am a great man," he proclaims. He is proud of his intellectual capabilities (his "little grey cells"), and maintains (in *The Mysterious Affair at Styles*) that, "I am not keeping back facts. Every fact that I know is in your possession. You can draw your own deductions from them." In 'The Kidnapped Prime Minister' (*Poirot Investigates*) he taps his forehead knowingly and exclaims, "The true clues are within – *here*!" He sneers at the Sherlock Holmes-type detective who rushes around the lawn measuring wet footprints in the grass, but he is known to do the same thing himself ('Dead Man's Mirror' – *Murder in the Mews*, 1937).

The only failure in his illustrious career occurred during his early days in the Belgian police force ('The Chocolate Box' – *Poirot Investigates*, 1924) in which he didn't notice the significance of a blue lid on a pink box. "My grey cells, they functioned not at all," he admits. From then on he asks Hastings to murmur "chocolate box" in his ear (cf "Norbury" in Arthur Conan Doyle's 'The Adventure of the Yellow Face') should he ever become conceited about his abilities.

He is not without subterfuge. His brother Achille makes an unexpected appearance in *The Big Four* – "Do you not know," Poirot says, "that all celebrated detectives have brothers who would be even more celebrated than they are, were it not for constitutional indolence?" – but it turns out that his sibling is not who he seems. In many early cases the detective says he has retired "to grow vegetable marrows", but apart from the one that he throws over the fence (accidentally) at his neighbour Dr Sheppard (*The Mysterious Affair at Styles*), we see little evidence of this hobby. He also claims he could make a good pickpocket ('The Wasps' Nest' – *Double Sin*, 1961*).

A man of leisure, he treats himself to many holidays. He travels abroad, occasionally accompanied by his manservant George (*The Mystery of the Blue Train*, 1928). He has visited such exotic locales as the Holy Land (*Appointment with Death*, 1938) and the Nile (*Death on the Nile*, 1937), and can sometimes be found staying at The Ritz (*Three Act Tragedy*, 1935). But there are also times when he mixes business with pleasure. He passes through Hassanieh, the dig site in Mesopotamia, on his way to Baghdad after "disentangling some military scandal in Syria" for the French government (*Murder in Mesopotamia*, 1936). He goes home on the Orient Express, and encounters another scandal that he must resolve (*Murder on the Orient Express*, 1934). Among his unrecorded cases is one involving M Blondin, proprietor of the Chez Ma Tante restaurant in London, which consisted of "a dead body… and a very lovely lady" (*Death on the Nile*).

His fame as a detective travels widely. M Fournier of the French Sûreté (*Death in the Clouds*, 1935) has heard of his reputation from M Giraud (*Murder on the Links*). He is quickly on the scene of a Yuletide murder because he has been staying nearby with the Chief Constable of Middleshire (*Hercule Poirot's Christmas*, 1938). And his presence is called to a case of poisoning because Dr John Stillingfleet ('The Dream' – *The Adventure of the Christmas Pudding*, 1960†) recommended him to Dr Peter Lord (*Sad Cypress*, 1940). But he realises that as he gets older, fewer and fewer people will have heard of him. He stops himself saying, "Most people have heard of me," when he realises those people are probably now residing in graveyards (*Elephants Can Remember*, 1972).

Poirot's idea of a perfect crime (*The ABC Murders*, 1936) would be one "with no complications" – in other words, no emotional entanglements, just a simple puzzle to solve. Such a case might involve four people in a closed room playing bridge while a fifth is murdered in full view of them – this is a prescient comment because the exact same situation occurs soon after (*Cards on the Table*, 1936). Inspector Japp says he'll end up detecting his own death, something he does indeed do (*Curtain: Poirot's Last Case*, 1975).

He enjoys children's verse, albeit reluctantly – "A jingle ran through Poirot's head. He repressed it. He must *not* always be thinking of nursery rhymes." (*Five Little Pigs*, 1943). On the other hand, his recollection of 'Rub A Dub Dub' helps him find a missing girl (*The Third Girl*, 1966). He knows 'Hickory Dickory Dock' and can quote easily from Lewis Carroll (*The Clocks*, 1963). As for 'serious' literature, he has a sound knowledge of English poetry, especially Tennyson (*The Hollow*), but misquotes Shakespeare (*Taken at the Flood*, 1948). Berating his lack of classical education, he indulges in a crash-course on ancient legends and then says he'll only solve more cases provided they conform to the twelve labours of his namesake Hercules (*The Labours of Hercules*, 1947). He forgets this promise soon after, and goes on to solve many more cases unlinked to classical mythology.

With regard to more contemporary reading matter (*The Clocks*), he recommends the following (real) murder mysteries: *The Leavenworth Case* (1878) by Anna Katherine Green, *The Adventures of Arsène Lupin* by Maurice Leblanc (1864–1941), and *The Mystery of the Yellow Room* (1908) by Gaston Leroux, but criticises the techniques of (fictional) crime writers Cyril Quain, Garry Gregson and Ariadne Oliver. Concerning Arthur Conan Doyle's *The Adventures of Sherlock Holmes* (1892), he just says, "Maître!" He is so well-read on the subject that he later publishes a critique of detective story writers (*The Third Girl*) in which he writes scathingly of Edgar Allan Poe and Wilkie Collins. He is typically proud of his book, despite the "really incredible number of printer's errors" contained in it.

As for culinary tastes, he considers himself a gourmet – he dines alone at a favourite Soho restaurant (*Mrs McGinty's Dead*, 1952). He is also known to enjoy a breakfast of brioche and hot chocolate (*Third Girl*). And he is certainly interested in the eating habits of others, especially when they lead to murder ('Four-and-Twenty Blackbirds' – *Three Blind Mice*, 1950*).

He admits that his oft-repeated remarks about retiring bear more than a passing resemblance to "the prima donna who makes positively that farewell performance" (*The ABC Murders*). But the moment does indeed arrive when he makes his very last curtain call. Confined to a wheelchair, his thin face lined and wrinkled, and sporting a false moustache and wig (*Curtain: Poirot's Last Case*), the incredibly aged Poirot admits that, "This, Hastings, will be my last case."

Captain Arthur Hastings

It was during his time working for Lloyds of London that Hastings met the retired Poirot in Belgium. In his thirties, he fought as an officer in the First World War, but in 1916 he was wounded in the Somme ('The Affair at the Victory Ball' – *The Under Dog*, 1951*) and was invalided out of the army. He had then spent several months in "a rather depressing Convalescent Home". Still on sick leave, he bumped into an old school friend, John Cavendish, who invited him to recuperate at Styles Court in Essex. After Cavendish's autocratic stepmother Mrs Inglethorp is found poisoned with strychnine, Hastings calls in his old friend Hercule Poirot who is coincidentally residing in the local village (*The Mysterious Affair at Styles*, 1920).

He has a small 'toothbrush' moustache (*Lord Edgware Dies*, 1933), and a propensity for redheads. He proposes to one such, Cynthia Murdoch (*The Mysterious Affair at Styles*), but is turned down. He turns to Dulcie Duveen next (*Murder on the Links*, 1923) and has more luck – the couple marry, he leaves his job as an MP's Private Secretary and they go off to the Argentine together. But he periodically returns to England to visit his old friend Poirot, leaving his wife to enjoy the "free and easy life of the South American continent". These enforced separations sometimes make him forget her name, and he once calls her Bella (*Peril at End House*, 1932), obviously getting her confused with her sister.

During the Depression he returns to England for six months to sort out his business affairs – as well as pick up an OBE – leaving his wife at home on their ranch (*The ABC Murders*, 1935). He likes dogs and takes a wire-haired terrier back to Argentina with him (*Dumb Witness*, 1937). Poirot claims he is too keen to put "the most romantic construction on every incident" ('The Mystery of the Spanish Chest' – *The Adventure of the Christmas Pudding*, 1960†).

A gap of many years follows – in which his place is filled by the efficient Miss Lemon – before he returns to help Poirot one final time (*Curtain: Poirot's Last Case*, 1975). His wife has died and he has four grown-up daughters, but all things considered he hasn't aged badly – after all this time he's still only in his fifties.

Appearances: Too numerous to mention.

Countess Vera Rossakoff

Flamboyant and overdressed Russian aristocrat with whom Poirot falls hopelessly in love – "What a woman!" he exclaims.

Appearances: *The Big Four* (1927), 'The Capture of Cerberus' (*The Labours of Hercules*, 1947) and 'Double Clue' (*Double Sin*, 1961*).

Chief Inspector James Japp

A "little, sharp, dark, ferret-faced" policeman who first worked with Poirot back in 1904 when the Belgian detective was still in the police force. They have remained good friends, despite having completely different crime solving methods – Poirot is methodical, while Japp follows his instincts. He has a tendency to refer to his friend as "Moosier Poirot".

Appearances: Too numerous to mention.

Colonel Johnny Race

A Secret Service operative described as "a dark, handsome, deeply bronzed man... usually to be found in some outpost of empire – especially if there were trouble brewing". He is in his sixties when we last see him.

Appearances: *The Man in the Brown Suit* (1924), *Cards on the Table* (1936), *Death on the Nile* (1937) and *Sparkling Cyanide* (1945).

Superintendent Battle

A large man with a stolid wooden face, he appears expressionless at all times, affecting an air of supreme unintelligence. But really he is very perceptive, and if you dig deep enough he has a heart of gold. He is said to work "almost entirely on cases of a delicate political nature". He appears conventional, yet holds some diverting views: "In my opinion all the people who spend their lives avoiding being run over by buses had much better be run over and put safely out of the way. They're no good."

Appearances: *The Secret of Chimneys* (1925), *The Seven Dials Mystery* (1929), *Cards on the Table* (1936), *Murder Is Easy* (1939) and *Towards Zero* (1944).

Ariadne Oliver

We first encounter this bestselling crime writer in 1936 and she goes on to become one of Poirot's closest friends. She has created a Finnish detective called Sven Hjerson, but regrets making him foreign: "I don't really know anything about Finns and I'm always getting letters from Finland pointing out something impossible that he's said or done." She is scatterbrained, untidy, and is always eating apples. She thinks the books she writes – such as *The Second Goldfish* and *The Body in the Library* – are "good of their kind". She hates politics, drinks *crème de menthe* (but prefers kirsch, a spirit distilled from wild cherries) and doesn't like fans – she never knows what to say to them.

As time goes on, she grows to hate her detective more. "If I met that bony, gangling, vegetable-eating Finn in real life, I'd do a better murder than any I've ever invented," she exclaims. Talented young playwright Robin Upward is adapting one of Mrs Oliver's novels for the stage, and suggests she writes a book to be published posthumously in which Hjerson is killed. Mrs Oliver declines, saying, "Any money to be made out of murders I want now."

In later life she possesses "wind-swept grey hair" and an "eagle profile" and by the time she goes solo to solve a case she has 55 murder mysteries under her belt. At the start of her last appearance she is called on to make a speech, something that is anathema to her. "You know I never make speeches!" she cries. "I get all worried and nervy and I should probably stammer or say the same thing twice... Now it's all right with words... I can do things with words so long as I know it's not a speech I'm making." To her publisher she says scornfully, "I don't believe *you* know whether anything I write is good or bad." Any similarity with another famous writer of detective fiction is, of course, *entirely* coincidental.

Appearances: 'The Case of the Discontented Soldier' and 'The Case of the Rich Woman' (*Parker Pyne Investigates*, 1934), *Cards on the Table* (1936), *Mrs McGinty's Dead* (1952), *Dead Man's Folly* (1956), *The Pale Horse* (1961), *Third Girl* (1966), *Hallowe'en Party* (1969) and *Elephants Can Remember* (1972).

Felicity Lemon

After first working as Parker Pyne's secretary (*Parker Pyne Investigates*, 1934), Miss Lemon fulfils the same rôle for Poirot when his friend Hastings returns to the Argentine for good. But unlike him, she is "very nearly the perfect machine, completely and gloriously uninterested in all human affairs" ('How Does Your Garden Grow?' – *The Regatta Mystery*, 1939*). Much to his delight, she rarely shows any emotion, her main goal in life being to perfect the ultimate filing system.

Appearances: Too numerous to mention.

1. The Mysterious Affair at Styles (1920)

Case: In a rambling country estate in Essex, a wealthy widow dies horribly of poison...

Context: Christie was an avid reader of Sherlock Holmes, and decided that her new detective would have to be completely different to him. She remembered a colony of Belgian war refugees that lived in Torquay and imagined one of them as a retired Belgian police officer; and since she envisioned him as being "a tidy little man", the name of Hercules – the strongman of Greek myth – seemed amusing to her. He does in fact bear some similarities with Holmes (especially his vanity), but one influence is hard to ignore: Belloc Lowndes, sister of Hilaire Belloc, had already created a vain French detective, retired from the Paris Sûreté, whose name was, oddly, Hercules Popeau. (As a further coincidence, in the mid-30s Lowndes wrote a Popeau story called *A Labour of Hercules*, uncannily similar to the title of Christie's 1947 collection.)

Christie finished her first novel on her sister's old typewriter and sent it to various publishers. In 1919, John Lane, managing director of The Bodley Head, told her that if she altered the courtroom denouement, they would publish it. She did, and signed a six-book deal with them, on rather unfair terms (subsidiary rights would be shared 50/50 between author and publisher and she would get no royalties until 2,000 copies were sold). She earned more money from its serialisation in *The Weekly Times* than she did on the book itself. While at The Bodley Head she acquired Edmund Cork (of Hughes Massie) as a literary agent, remaining with the firm until her death 50 years later.

Conclusion: Everything that made Christie so popular is already in place here, and although some of the characterisation is a little stilted, the book is an accomplished debut. **5/5**

2. Murder on the Links (1923)

Case: On a French golf course a millionaire is found stabbed in the back...

Context: Christie argued with The Bodley Head over the cover illustration, claiming it was badly drawn and misleading (the victim was dressed in pyjamas and having an epileptic fit rather than being stabbed and wearing an overcoat); from then on, she got first approval. The story was apparently inspired by a French murder in which a masked intruder broke into a house, killed a man and tied up his wife – but discrepancies led to the wife being suspected. Christie thought it "a moderately good example of its kind".

Conclusion: A cunning murder puzzle with plenty of style. **4/5**

3. Poirot Investigates (1924, ss)

Cases:

'The Adventure of the Western Star': A film star receives threatening letters about her diamond...

'The Tragedy at Marsdon Manor': A bankrupt businessman is found dead in a field...

'The Adventure of the Cheap Flat': A posh apartment is being rented for a ridiculously low sum...

'The Mystery of Hunter's Lodge': A wealthy uncle is murdered in his nephew's hunting lodge...

'The Million-Dollar Bond Robbery': Liberty bonds have disappeared from a locked trunk...

'The Adventure of the Egyptian Tomb': An archaeologist dies after a pharaoh's curse...

'The Jewel Robbery at the Grand Metropolitan': French hotel maids are accused of stealing some valuable pearls...

'The Kidnapped Prime Minister': Enemy agents abduct the head of the government...

'The Disappearance of Mr Davenheim': A banker never returns from posting a letter...

'The Adventure of the Italian Nobleman': An Italian count is bludgeoned to death with a statuette...

'The Case of the Missing Will': If a young woman finds her uncle's will, she inherits his estate...

'The Veiled Lady' (US): A titled woman is plagued by a blackmailer...

'The Lost Mine' (US): A Chinese mine-owner is found floating in the Thames...

'The Chocolate Box' (US): Years ago a French deputy was found poisoned in Belgium...

Context: Christie produced most of these stories for the illustrated London weekly *The Sketch* in 1923 (but she thought that W Smithson Broadhead's illustration of Poirot was too dandified). The working title was *The Grey Cells of Monsieur Poirot*. The last three stories were only in the American edition of the book, appearing in the UK fifty years later in *Poirot's Early Cases* (1974).

Conclusion: An engaging selection. **4/5**

4. The Murder of Roger Ackroyd (1926)

Case: In the quiet village of King's Abbot a wealthy widower is found stabbed to death in his study...

Context: The basic idea for this book – the first one published by Collins in the UK – was given to her by her brother-in-law James Watts, allegedly backed up by Lord Louis Mountbatten. The *Daily Sketch* called it "the best thriller ever", while the *News Chronicle* thought it "a tasteless and unfortunate let-down by a writer we had grown to admire". Christie admitted that the character of Caroline Sheppard was the direct antecedent of Miss Marple.

Conclusion: An absolute masterpiece, the book simply takes one's breath away with its audacity. **5/5**

5. The Big Four (1927)

Case: A ruthless international cartel seeks world domination...

Context: Twelve stories from the magazine *The Sketch* were strung together to form the semblance of a full-length novel, with Archie's brother Campbell helping Christie with the rewriting. Chapter 11, 'A Chess Problem', has appeared separately in various anthologies. Increased sales of the book were arguably due to the author's disappearance a few months earlier.

Conclusion: A contrived attempt to drop Poirot into a loosely structured espionage thriller. **3/5**

6. The Mystery of the Blue Train (1928)

Case: The daughter of an American millionaire dies on a train en route to Nice...

Context: Based on the short story 'The Plymouth Express' (*Poirot's Early Cases*, 1974), Christie thought it the worst book she ever wrote. But she later said that it marked the point where she changed from an amateur to a professional, as it was the first time she had written for money rather than pleasure.

Conclusion: A good Poirot tale with the requisite amount of false clues and red herrings. **4/5**

7. Peril at End House (1932)

Case: In a lonely house on a cliff-top, a young woman fears for her life...

Context: The action, although taking place in the fictional Cornish town of St Loo, is clearly based on her hometown of Torquay in Devon. The fictional Majestic Hotel is a thinly disguised version of the imposing Imperial Hotel.

Conclusion: Not the most exciting book she wrote, but still ingenious in its own way. **3/5**

8. Lord Edgware Dies (1933)

Case: An estranged husband is found stabbed to death in his own library...

Context: The character of Carlotta Adams is based on an American entertainer called Ruth Draper (1884–1956) who could change her appearance with a minimum of props. At one point Poirot is called away to solve the case of 'The Ambassador's Boots', a crime actually solved by Tommy and Tuppence in *Partners in Crime* (1929).

Conclusion: Brilliantly plotted with a dazzling array of upper-class characters. **5/5**

9. Murder on the Orient Express (1934)

Case: A wealthy American dies of multiple stab wounds on a train bound for Paris...

Context: Christie was inspired to write this story after travelling on the Simplon-Orient Express to Iraq in 1933. After writing the novel at the archaeological dig at Arpachiyah, she double-checked her facts on the journey home. It was based on a tragic case a year earlier, when the son of noted aviator Charles Lindbergh was kidnapped and killed. The American title was changed to *Murder in the Calais Coach* to avoid confusion with Graham Greene's 1932 novel *Stamboul Train*, published there as *Orient Express*. Dorothy L Sayers in *The Sunday Times* described Christie's book as "a murder mystery conceived and carried out on the finest classical lines".

Conclusion: The archetypal Christie – claustrophobia, paranoia, and everyone a suspect. Great stuff. **5/5**

10. Three Act Tragedy (1935)

Case: At an apparently respectable dinner party, a vicar is the first to die...

Context: This book is presented in the form of a play, with mock theatre credits at the front. Mr Satterthwaite (from the Harley Quin stories) appears as a supporting player. It became the first Christie story to sell more than 10,000 copies within its first year of publication.

Conclusion: Characters are not so well defined as usual, and the dénouement is an anticlimax. **2/5**

11. Death in the Clouds (1935)

Case: A woman is killed by a poisoned dart in the enclosed confines of a commercial biplane...

Context: Air travel was still a novelty when Christie wrote this

aeronautical mystery, which she set aboard an HP42 Hannibal-class biplane. Christie satirises her own profession in the character of Daniel Clancy, creator of fictional detective Wilbraham Rice: a "scribbler of rubbish," says Japp. An authorial error in the first chapter puts the passengers in the rear compartment, rather than the forward one.
Conclusion: Good period flavour and an intriguing puzzle to solve. **4/5**

12. The ABC Murders (1936)

Case: An alphabetically-obsessed serial killer is on the loose...
Context: The novel was serialised by the *Daily Express* in 1935, with readers invited to submit their solutions. The plot of *Cards on the Table* (1936) is outlined in Chapter 3. Many writers have used the novel as a springboard for their own stories, notably Elizabeth Linington's *Greenmask!* (1964), Ellery Queen's *Cat of Many Tails* (1949) and Sebastien Japrisot's *The Sleeping Car Murders* (1963).
Conclusion: A tightly plotted and brilliantly executed serial killer whodunit. **5/5**

13. Murder in Mesopotamia (1936)

Case: An archaeologist's wife is murdered on the shores of the river Tigris...
Context: The murder victim Louise Leidner is similar to the real-life Katherine Woolley, the dominating wife of the leader of the dig at Ur in 1929/30. Christie's husband Max was Woolley's assistant, he himself allegedly inspired the quiet assistant archaeologist David Emmott.
Conclusion: Entertaining, albeit far-fetched. **4/5**

14. Cards on the Table (1936)

Case: A Mephistophelian party host is murdered in full view of a roomful of bridge players...
Context: Ariadne Oliver makes her first appearance here. Spoiler alert: the solution to *The Murder on The Orient Express* (1934) is casually mentioned in passing.
Conclusion: Christie's most dialogue-heavy novel, it sags alarmingly in the middle. **2/5**

15. Murder in the Mews (1937, ss)

Cases:
'Murder in the Mews': A widow is murdered in her apartment...
'The Incredible Theft': Secret bomber plans have been stolen during a ministerial conference...
'Dead Man's Mirror': An eccentric peer is found dead in his library, next to a shattered mirror...
'Triangle at Rhodes': A complicated ménage à trois develops on a Greek island holiday...
Context: 'Murder in the Mews' was a revised version of 'The Market Basing Mystery', later collected in *The Under Dog* (1951*). Similarly, 'The Incredible Theft' was an expanded version of 'The Submarine Plans' (also to be found in *The Under Dog*) and was omitted from the US version of this collection, entitled *Dead Man's Mirror*. 'Dead Man's Mirror' itself, in which Mr Satterthwaite from the Harley Quin stories appears, was a longer version of 'The Second Gong', later found in *The Witness for the Prosecution* (1948*).
Conclusion: Interesting to compare the first three stories with their embryonic forerunners. 3/5

16. Dumb Witness (1937)

Case: An elderly spinster has been poisoned in her country home...
Context: A dog plays a major part in this story, and the book is dedicated to Christie's own terrier, Peter. Expanded from an unpublished short story called *The Incident of the Dog's Ball* (only available on audio), the opening is based on 'How Does Your Garden Grow?' from *Poirot's Early Cases* (1974). Spoiler alert: in Chapter 18, Poirot mentions the murderers in the following four novels: *The Mysterious Affair at Styles* (1920), *The Murder of Roger Ackroyd* (1926), *The Mystery of the Blue Train* (1928) and *Death in the Clouds* (1935)!
Conclusion: A run-of-the-mill mystery, with mawkish anthropomorphism. 2/5

17. Death on the Nile (1937)

Case: The heir to a fortune is murdered aboard an Egyptian river steamer...
Context: Christie considered this "one of the best" of her foreign travel novels, the geographical and historical details all picked up on her various Egyptian trips. Sadly, nowadays almost everything mentioned

in the book is submerged under the waters of Lake Nasser, apart from the temple of Ramses II – which was moved further up the mountain to safety – and the Cataract Hotel, now called the Old Cataract (a new one stands beside it).

Conclusion: Expertly plotted and set against a vivid and exotic backdrop, this is one of Christie's most entertaining reads. **5/5**

18. Appointment with Death (1938)

Case: A repugnant American widow is killed in Petra...

Context: Christie visited Petra in 1933, using the distinctive terrain for this and one other story ('The Pearl of Price' from *Parker Pyne Investigates*, 1934). The domineering American MP Lady Westholme is a parody of American-born MP and political hostess Lady Nancy Astor (1879–1964), the first woman to sit in the House of Commons.

Conclusion: Another colourful story populated with plenty of likely suspects and set against a moody, mysterious backdrop. Only the ending disappoints. **4/5**

19. Hercule Poirot's Christmas (1938)

Case: A sadistic old man is brutally murdered in his locked study...

Context: This is a traditional English country house murder mystery mixed with a John Dickson Carr-style locked room puzzle. Spoiler alert: In Part 3, Chapter 5, the murderer in *Three Act Tragedy* is casually revealed. In a 1938 *Daily Mail* interview, Christie said this about Poirot: "There are moments when I have felt: 'Why – why – why did I ever invent this detestable, bombastic, tiresome little creature?'"

Conclusion: Despite Christie's misgivings about her title character, the plot ranks as one of her best. **5/5**

20. The Regatta Mystery (1939*, ss)

Cases:

'The Mystery of the Baghdad Chest': A man disappears just before a party is thrown...

'How Does Your Garden Grow?': An elderly woman seeks Poirot's help and then dies...

'Yellow Iris': In a nightclub, people commemorate the death of a poisoned friend...

'The Dream': A reclusive millionaire is plagued by suicidal nightmares...

'Problem at Sea': A liner's passenger is discovered with a dagger in her heart…

Context: 'The Mystery of the Baghdad Chest' was later expanded to almost twice its length and retitled 'The Mystery of the Spanish Chest' for inclusion in *The Adventure of the Christmas Pudding* (1960†). The beginning of 'How Does Your Garden Grow?' is similar to *Dumb Witness* (1937). 'Yellow Iris' formed the basis for the Poirot-less novel *Sparkling Cyanide* (1945). 'Problem at Sea' is also known as 'The Mystery of the Crime in Cabin 66' and was also published, under the title 'Crime in Cabin 66', as a 16–page booklet in 1944, by the Vallency Press.

Conclusion: A nice collection of Poirot mysteries. **4/5**

21. Sad Cypress (1940)

Case: An elderly stroke victim dies intestate…

Context: The title is a quotation from *Twelfth Night*, referring to the subject matter of old age and euthanasia. Christie later said the book was "ruined by having Poirot in it".

Conclusion: A bleak book, this is probably the most realistic, least plot-driven of Christie's crime stories. **3/5**

22. One, Two, Buckle My Shoe (1940)

Case: A dentist lies murdered at his Harley Street practice…

Context: Each chapter corresponds loosely to a line of the famous nursery line. Set just before the outbreak of World War Two, there are many references to events and people in the real world, such as Hitler, Mussolini, Oswald Mosley's blackshirts and the IRA.

Conclusion: Complicated, rather than complex, this is a little too far-fetched to be entirely satisfying. **3/5**

23. Evil Under the Sun (1941)

Case: A beautiful woman is strangled to death on a remote beach…

Context: Various Devon locations appear in this book. Torquay is called St Loo, the fictional Smuggler's Island is Bigbury-on-Sea's Burgh Island (used again in *Ten Little Niggers*, 1939), the town itself is renamed Leathercombe, and the annual Torquay Regatta fireworks are mentioned, as they were in *Peril at End House* (1932). With its 'eternal triangle' theme, the story shares similarities with *Death on the Nile* (1937).

Conclusion: Another excellent whodunit with a fiendishly clever resolution. **5/5**

24. Five Little Pigs (1943)

Case: A womanising painter was poisoned sixteen years ago by his wife, but now his daughter believes she was innocent all along...

Context: Some of artist Amyas Crale's less pleasant traits may have been borrowed from real-life painter Augustus John. The events of the novel are set in 1926, the year of Christie's disappearance, and seem to mirror Archie leaving her for Nancy Neele. It was the first book to sell 20,000 in its first edition. Crale's house is modelled on the author's Devon home of Greenway House.

Conclusion: With its vivid characterisation and strong plot, this is the first and best of Christie's 'murder in retrospect' novels. **5/5**

25. Poirot Knows the Murderer (1946, ss)

'The Mystery of the Baghdad Chest': See *The Regatta Mystery* (1939*). 'The Mystery of the Crime in Cabin 66': Ditto (an alternative title for 'Problem at Sea').

26. Poirot Lends a Hand (1946, ss)

'The Veiled Lady': See *Poirot Investigates* (1924).

27. The Hollow (1946)

Case: A young doctor has been shot in broad daylight by his jealous wife...

Context: *The Hollow* was modelled on Poirot actor Francis L Sullivan's home in Haslemere, Surrey. During one of Christie's weekend stays there during the war, she paced around the garden and swimming pool to work out the intricacies of the plot. Like *Sad Cypress* (1940), Christie regretted the inclusion of Poirot and omitted him from her stage adaptation.

Conclusion: Another brilliantly plotted exercise, this time with stronger characterisation than usual. **5/5**

28. The Labours of Hercules (1947, ss)

Cases: 'The Nemean Lion': A Pekinese dog is 'dognapped' and held for ransom...
'The Lernean Hydra': Gossipmongers are accusing a doctor of poisoning his wife...
'The Arcadian Deer': A garage mechanic falls in love with a lady's maid...
'The Erymanthian Boar': An underworld gang-leader is chased into the Alps...
'The Augean Stables': A gutter-press newspaper is flinging mud at a prime minister...
'The Stymphalean Birds': Female blackmailers in Herzoslovakia are stirring up trouble...
'The Cretan Bull': A woman's boyfriend appears to be going mad...
'The Horses of Diomedes': Four wild young daughters get mixed up in a world of drugs...
'The Girdle of Hyppolita': An exclusive Parisian finishing school holds the key to a stolen Rubens painting...
'The Flock of Geryon': A group of woman have been brainwashed by a dangerous cult...
'The Apples of the Hesperides': An Italian renaissance goblet goes missing...
'The Capture of Cerberus': A dope ring operates out of a subterranean nightclub...
Context: Poirot says he will solve only twelve more cases, provided they correspond with the labours of Greek hero Hercules.
Conclusion: This is probably the best Poirot collection because of its clever linking theme and the witty interpretation of modern-day life into classical myth. **5/5**

29. Taken at the Flood (1948)

Case: A man returns from the dead and the body of a mysterious stranger is found in his room...
Context: The title is taken from Brutus' speech in *Julius Caesar* (act IV, scene iii). The character of Enoch Arden (who shares his name with the title of Tennyson's narrative poem) also crops up in one of Christie's earlier short stories, 'While the Light Lasts' (from the 1997 UK collection), which forms the basis for this novel. The Furrowbank Estate at Warmsley Vale is based on Archie and

Christie's old country house near Sunningdale golf course.

Conclusion: Blending post-war realism with a domestic murder mystery, this offers an interesting slant on a fairly standard story. **4/5**

30. The Witness for the Prosecution (1948*, ss)

Case: 'The Second Gong': An eccentric peer has been shot in his library...

Context: This is an early version of the novella 'Dead Man's Mirror' from *Murder in the Mews* (1937). The plot and characters are similar, but names and ending differ.

Conclusion: Passable Poirot. **3/5**

31. Three Blind Mice and Other Stories (1950*, ss)

Cases: 'The Third Floor Flat': Two young couples find a body in their apartment building...

'The Adventure of Johnnie Waverly': The son of a steel magnate has been kidnapped...

'Four-and-Twenty Blackbirds': A man's altered eating habits leads to a trail of murder...

Context: 'The Adventure of Johnnie Waverly' is also known as 'The Kidnapping of Johnnie Waverly'.

Conclusion: An engaging trio. **4/5**

32. The Under Dog and Other Stories (1951*, ss)

Cases: 'The Under Dog': An irascible financier is bludgeoned to death in his tower retreat...

'The Plymouth Express'; The body of a millionaire's daughter is found stuffed under a train seat... 'The Affair at the Victory Ball': A society playboy is stabbed in the heart while his fiancée dies of a cocaine overdose...

'The Market Basing Mystery': A village recluse is found shot through the head...

'The Lemesurier Inheritance': A family's firstborn sons are dying off because of an old family curse...

'The Cornish Mystery': A wife fears her husband is trying to poison her...

'The King of Clubs': A prince's fiancée is involved in the murder of a stage impresario...

'The Submarine Plans': Secret plans have been stolen during a ministerial conference...

'The Case of the Clapham Cook': An employer wants to find her missing domestic...

Context: These stories were all published in British magazines from 1923 to 1926, three of them later extended to make longer narratives: 'The Plymouth Express', much expanded, became *The Mystery of the Blue Train* (1928), 'The Market Basing Mystery' became 'Murder in the Mews' (the title story of the 1937 collection) and 'The Submarine Plans' formed the basis of 'The Incredible Theft', from the same collection. 'The Affair at the Victory Ball', which follows on directly from events in *The Mysterious Affair at Styles* (1920), appears to be the earliest Poirot short story.

Conclusion: A mixed bag of stories. 3/5

33. Mrs McGinty's Dead (1952)

Case: An old widow is killed in the parlour of her cottage...

Context: Crime writer Ariadne Oliver returns after a 16–year absence to provide a mouth-piece for Christie on the woes of adapting her works for the stage; ironically the book was dedicated to Peter Saunders, producer of *The Mousetrap* (1952).

Conclusion: Unusually for a Poirot story, this has a lower middle class setting, which works very well. 5/5

34. After the Funeral (1953)

Case: The master of a Victorian mansion dies suddenly – and his sister thinks it was murder...

Context: The fictional Enderby Hall is based on a home that Christie's sister Madge and her husband James Watts lived in – a huge Victorian house called Abney Hall in Cheadle, near Manchester. She spent her childhood Christmases there (it features in the title story of *The Adventure of the Christmas Pudding*, 1960†) and it was the place in which she chose to lie low after her 1926 disappearance. The book has the first and only use of a family tree to help understand the complicated relationships.

Conclusion: After the realism of her other post-war fiction, Christie goes back into the past for this rose-tinted nostalgia trip. 3/5

35. Hickory Dickory Dock (1955)

Case: Odd things are happening in a youth hostel…

Context: The title, one of many nursery rhyme references used by Christie, has nothing to do with this story, despite it being set in Hickory Road. There are echoes of 'The Ambassador's Boots' from the Tommy and Tuppence collection *Partners in Crime* (1929); Evelyn Waugh in his diaries called it "twaddle".

Conclusion: A partially successful attempt to move away from cosy country murders to the squalor of 1950s student London. **3/5**

36. Dead Man's Folly (1956)

Case: A charity 'murder hunt' turns into the real thing…

Context: In 1954 Christie wrote the novella *Hercule Poirot and the Greenshore Folly*, intending to use the proceeds to fund a new stained-glass window in her local church. Unable to find a publisher, she instead expanded the plot into this novel. The original novella was finally published in 2014. The fictional Nasse House is based on Greenway in Devon, the house Christie bought in 1939 (its boathouse is where the corpse is found). The nearby village of Galmpton features as Nassecombe, and the Maypool Youth Hostel becomes the Hoodown Youth Hostel. This is one of only two occasions when Christie kills off a child.

Conclusion: Good, traditional fare. **4/5**

37. Cat Among the Pigeons (1959)

Case: Unpleasant things are going on in an exclusive school for girls…

Context: Set in the girls' school of Meadowbank, some critics have compared it to Josephine Tey's *Miss Pym Disposes* (1946), although the plots are quite dissimilar. The enigmatic Mr Robinson, a member of a financial syndicate called the Arrangers, also appears in a Marple novel (*At Bertram's Hotel*, 1956), a Tommy and Tuppence novel (*Postern of Fate*, 1973) and a thriller (*Passenger to Frankfurt*, 1970), making him the only person to feature with all of Christie's major detectives.

Conclusion: There are signs that Christie's magic formula is wearing a bit thin. **2/5**

38. The Adventure of the Christmas Pudding and a Selection of Entrées (1960†, ss)

Cases: 'The Adventure of the Christmas Pudding': A valuable ruby ends up in a country house...

'The Mystery of the Spanish Chest': A man disappears just before a party is thrown...

'The Under Dog': See *The Under Dog* (1951*).

'Four-and-Twenty Blackbirds': See *Three Blind Mice* (1950*).

'The Dream': See *The Regatta Mystery* (1939*).

Context: For reasons unknown, Christie didn't produce a new book for 1960; instead Collins took the one new title story (a longer version of 'Christmas Adventure' as found in *When the Light Lasts*, 1997†) and added five others to it. 'The Mystery of the Spanish Chest' is an expanded version of 'The Mystery of the Baghdad Chest' which had first appeared in *The Regatta Mystery* (1939*) – Hastings is replaced in this newer version by Miss Lemon.

Conclusion: An unremarkable couple of stories. **3/5**

39. Double Sin and Other Stories (1961*)

Cast: 'Double Sin': Valuable miniatures have been stolen from a train...

'The Wasps' Nest': Poirot investigates a murder before it has taken place...

'The Theft of the Royal Ruby': See *The Adventure of the Christmas Pudding* (1960†) – this is an alternative name for the title story.

'The Double Clue': A prized collection of medieval jewels are stolen from a safe...

Context: These stories were first published in magazines from 1923 to 1928.

Conclusion: A reasonable selection. **4/5**

40. Thirteen For Luck! (US: 1961, UK: 1966, ss)

'Double Sin': See *Double Sin* (1961*).

'The Arcadian Deer': See *The Labours of Hercules* (1947).

'The Adventure of Johnnie Waverly': See *Three Blind Mice* (1950*).

'The Third Floor Flat': Ditto.

'The Plymouth Express': See *The Under Dog* (1951*).

'The Cornish Mystery': Ditto.

41. The Clocks (1963)

Case: A typist discovers a man's body behind a sofa...

Context: Unique in having two virtually unrelated plots, this novel also sees an atypical blending of espionage and crime detection (as in *The Big Four*, 1927).

Conclusion: The promising set-up seems to get lost in the cut and thrust of the plot, but it's by no means the worst latter-day Christie. **3/5**

42. Third Girl (1966)

Case: A perplexed girl thinks she *may* have killed someone...

Context: Sex, drugs and hippies populate this thirtieth Poirot novel, one in which the detective admits he is finally growing old.

Conclusion: Interesting to see how the elderly Christie viewed the 'swinging sixties'. **3/5**

43. Hallowe'en Party (1969)

Case: A teenage murder witness is drowned in a tub of apples...

Context: This is only the second Christie novel to feature the death of a child. The house of Apple Trees is modelled on Christie's childhood home Ashfield, in particular the toilet halfway up the stairs. For the first and only time Christie uses the word 'lesbian' in a book, although she clearly wrote about such a couple in the Miss Marple story *A Murder is Announced* (1950).

Conclusion: Not on a par with her earlier books maybe, but still much to enjoy. **3/5**

44. Elephants Can Remember (1972)

Case: An old husband and wife 'double murder' has never properly been solved – until now...

Context: This is the last Poirot story that Christie ever wrote. The premise is taken from an earlier short story, 'Greenshaw's Folly' (*The Adventure of the Christmas Pudding*, 1960†). There are many internal errors and inconsistencies, due no doubt to the author's advancing age, but it garnered some good reviews, such as *The Birmingham Post*'s comment: "A beautiful example of latter-day Christie."

Conclusion: Nothing happens, and no-one can remember anything. As a short story it would have worked, as a novel it's sheer tedium. **1/5**

45. Poirot's Early Cases (1974, ss)

'The Lost Mine': See the US version of *Poirot Investigates* (1924).
'The Chocolate Box': Ditto.
'The Veiled Lady': Ditto.
'Problem at Sea': See *The Regatta Mystery* (1939*).
'How Does Your Garden Grow?': Ditto.
'The Adventure of Johnnie Waverly': See *Three Blind Mice* (1950*).
'The Third Floor Flat': Ditto.
'The Affair at the Victory Ball': See *The Under Dog* (1951*).
'The Adventure of the Clapham Cook': Ditto.
'The Cornish Mystery': Ditto.
'The King of Clubs': Ditto.
'The Lemesurier Inheritance': Ditto.
'The Plymouth Express': Ditto.
'The Submarine Plans': Ditto.
'The Market Basing Mystery': Ditto.
'The Double Clue': See *Double Sin* (1961*).
'Double Sin': Ditto.
'The Wasps' Nest': Ditto.

46. Curtain: Poirot's Last Case (1975)

Case: A wheelchair-bound Poirot returns to Styles Court where he knows a murder will shortly take place…

Context: Sir William Collins asked Christie to publish a manuscript she'd written during World War Two that described Poirot's final adventure. She'd intended to hold this back until after her death (assigning the rights to her daughter Rosalind) but was persuaded to release it early when it became clear she wouldn't produce a new book for Christmas 1975 – a first edition of 120,000 sold out straight away. Due to the early writing date, Poirot seems more youthful – despite being an invalid – than he is in *Elephants Can Remember* (1972).

Conclusion: A nostalgic flashback to the 1940s, this is a sombre mystery story with a good surprise ending (albeit rather an unconvincing one). 4/5

47. Problem at Pollensa Bay and Other Stories (1991†, ss)

'The Second Gong': See *The Witness for the Prosecution* (1948*).

48. While the Light Lasts (1997†, ss)

Cases: 'The Mystery of the Baghdad Chest': See *The Regatta Mystery* (1939*).
'Christmas Adventure': A ruby finds its way to a country house at Christmas.
Context: The latter story was expanded to become 'The Adventure of the Christmas Pudding' in the 1960 collection of the same name.
Conclusion: A slight tale with a few amusing moments. 3/5

49. The Harlequin Tea Set (1997*, ss)

'The Mystery of the Spanish Chest': See *The Adventure of the Christmas Pudding* (1960†).

50. Hercule Poirot and the Greenshore Folly (2000)

Case: In rural Devon, a treasure hunt becomes a murder hunt for M Poirot...
Context: This posthumously published novella formed the basis for *Dead Man's Folly* (1956)
Conclusion: A quick read, for completists only.

5

Miss Jane Marple

12 novels, 20 short stories

Jane Marple

Described by her friend Dolly Bantry as "the typical old maid of fiction" (*The Thirteen Problems*, 1932), Miss Marple is an elderly spinster who has lived most of her life in the village of St Mary Mead, about 25 miles from London. When she was young she spent some time in a pensionnat (boarding house) in Florence (*They Do It With Mirrors*, 1952).

She is first described as wearing "a black brocade dress... black lace mittens, and a black lace cap [which] surmounted the piled-up masses of her snowy hair" (*The Thirteen Problems*). Her later appearance is toned down to a less stern "white-haired old lady with a gentle, appealing manner" (*The Murder at the Vicarage*, 1930).

From the vantage point of her much-loved garden, she can see everything that goes on around her and considers herself an amateur sleuth of some ability. Prior to her first murder case, she has only solved mundane puzzles, among them the disappearance of Miss Wetherby's gill of pickled shrimps and the theft of the Church Boys' Outing money by the organist. She is confident that she can solve more serious mysteries by extrapolating her experiences of village life to bigger issues. She quotes a saying of her Great Aunt Fanny: "The young people think the old people are fools; but the old people *know* the young people are fools!" At one point Chief Constable Melchett says, "I really believe that wizened-up old maid thinks she knows everything there is to know. And hardly been out of this village all her life. Preposterous. What can she know of life?" But the local vicar replies that though Miss Marple may know next to nothing of Life with a capital L, she knows practically everything that goes on in St Mary Mead – and a surprising amount of murder and scandal there is too (*The Murder at the Vicarage*).

When she solves her first case, she is quite happy that the honour goes to Inspector Slack – her place is behind the scenes. Sir Henry Clithering says of her: "She's just the finest detective God ever made. Natural genius cultivated in a suitable soil." She's also a tough nut – of a murderer she declares, "I feel quite pleased to think of [him] being hanged" (*The Body in the Library*, 1942).

When she investigates a murder on a train for her friend Mrs McGillicuddy (*4.50 from Paddington*, 1957) she claims to be nearly ninety, but despite this decrepitude she can slip "with incredible swiftness" from a villain's grasp. In a later case she has had a fall and is taking things easy – until a murder occurs (*The Mirror Crack'd from Side to Side*, 1962). By this time she is too elderly to do anything in her garden other than "a little light pruning" and remembers fondly when her eyesight was good and she could keep an eye on the village goings-on. This will be the last time she is seen in St Mary Mead – it seems that she doesn't like the way village life is going and wants to get as far away from it as possible.

For one thing, she believes people talk about sex too much nowadays and therefore trivialise it – there was plenty of it around in her youth, but its secrecy made it exciting. And she is well aware of what goes on in the real world nowadays: "Plenty of sex, natural and unnatural," she says with certainty. "Rape, incest, perversion of all kinds."

She is much perkier on a Caribbean holiday paid for by her nephew Raymond (*A Caribbean Mystery*, 1964). Even at her advanced age she gets round easily and even sneaks through a flowerbed to eavesdrop on a suspect. Another trip to an old-fashioned London hotel (*At Bertram's Hotel*, 1965) seems to rejuvenate her even more, and by the time of her penultimate case (*Nemesis*, 1971) she is described as being "seventy if she is a day – nearer eighty perhaps". Concerning her unerring ability to be in the thick of things, she admits, "I have never read books on criminology as a subject or really been interested in such a thing. No, it has just happened that I have found myself in the vicinity of murder rather more often than would seem normal."

Her final recorded case (*Sleeping Murder*, 1976) has all the hallmarks of being a flashback to the 1940s. The years have rolled away and she is described as "an attractive old lady, tall and thin, with pink cheeks and blues eyes and a gentle, rather fussy manner." Once she has successfully closed the case, we can imagine this more youthful Jane Marple going on to solve many more puzzling mysteries.

Colonel Arthur and Dolly Bantry

Both are firm friends of Miss Marple. To begin with Dolly thinks Miss Marple is hopelessly behind the times, but then several years later she asks her, "Why don't you come out boldly and call yourself a criminologist and have done with it?" By this time, 1962, the Colonel has died and his wife has sold her home, Gossington Hall, to the glamorous movie star Marina Gregg (although he returns from the dead in Miss Marple's final case).

Appearances: *The Thirteen Problems* (1932), *The Body in the Library* (1942), *The Mirror Crack'd from Side to Side* (1962) and *Sleeping Murder* (1976).

Reverend Leonard and Griselda Clement

Seemingly ill-suited husband and wife, he middle-aged and set in his ways, she young and slightly scatty. They have an infant who crawls backwards.

Appearances: *The Murder at the Vicarage* (1930) and *The Body in the Library* (1942).

Sir Henry Clithering

Ex-Commissioner of Scotland Yard who holds a special respect for Miss Marple's talents.

Appearances: *The Thirteen Problems* (1932), *The Body in the Library* (1942) and *A Murder is Announced* (1950).

Chief Inspector Dermot Craddock

The nephew and godson of Sir Henry Clithering, he is thorough, intelligent and has enough imagination to keep an open mind until the very end of a case. At first he was wary of Miss Marple's methods but by his last appearance he had grown to trust and admire her.

Appearances: *A Murder is Announced* (1950), *4.50 from Paddington* (1957), *The Mirror Crack'd from Side to Side* (1962) and 'Sanctuary' (*Double Sin*,1961*).

Dr Haydock

Miss Marple's own doctor and the local police surgeon. A flawed humanitarian, he is upright and above suspicion.

Appearances: *The Murder at the Vicarage* (1930), *The Body in the Library* (1942) and 'The Case of the Caretaker' (*Three Blind Mice*, 1950*).

Colonel Melchett

Chief Constable of Radfordshire.

Appearances: *The Murder at the Vicarage* (1930) and 'The Tape-Measure Murder' (*Three Blind Mice*, 1950*).

Inspector Slack

Rude and overbearing, he is universally disliked by all those he comes into contact with. He denigrates Miss Marple, even though she is the one who provides the solutions to the mysteries.

Appearances: *The Murder at the Vicarage* (1930), *The Body in the Library* (1942), 'The Tape-Measure Murder' and 'The Case of the Perfect Maid' (both *Three Blind Mice*, 1950*).

Raymond & Joyce West

Raymond is "a modern novelist who dealt with strong meat in his books, incest, sex, and sordid descriptions of bedrooms and lavatory equipment" (*The Thirteen Problems*, 1932). He is Miss Marple's nephew; she dislikes his books but basks in the reflected glow of his reputation. He, on the other hand, treats her with a patronising kindness, thinking she knows nothing of the real world. He is married to Joyce Lemprière, a young modern painter with a "close-cropped black head and queer hazel-green eyes" and they have two children, his second son David working for British Railways. He tries to persuade Miss Marple to read modern novels but she says they're "all about such unpleasant people, doing such very odd things and not, apparently, even enjoying them."

Appearances: *The Murder at the Vicarage* (1930), *The Thirteen Problems* (1932), 'Miss Marple Tells a Story' (*The Regatta Mystery*, 1939*), 'Greenshaw's Folly' (*The Adventure of the Christmas Pudding*, 1960*), *A Caribbean Mystery* (1964), *Bertram's Hotel* (1965) and *Sleeping Murder* (1976).

1. The Murder at the Vicarage (1930)

Case: An unpopular colonel is found shot through the head in the vicar's study...

Context: Christie wanted to appeal to women readers when she introduced 'old pussy' Miss Marple. The character was inspired by a number of sources. Firstly, from Caroline Sheppard in *The Murder of Roger Ackroyd* (1926) – Christie said that Caroline was "an acidulated spinster, full of curiosity, knowing everything, hearing everything – the complete detective in the home." Secondly, from Miss Amelia Butterworth, the elderly spinster detective created by Anna Katharine Green (1846–1935) and introduced in *That Affair Next Door* (1897); Christie had read at least one of Green's detective books when she was a child. Thirdly, as a composite of her grandmother, who always saw the worst side of human nature, and her "Ealing cronies" – old ladies she'd met in many different villages she'd visited as a child.

In her autobiography, Christie says, "Miss Marple was born at the age of sixty-five to seventy – which, as with Poirot, proved unfortunate because she was going to have to last a long time in my life." Christie later considered *The Murder at the Vicarage* to have too many characters and too many subplots, and Bruce Rae in the *New York Times* said: "It will add little to her eminence in the field of detective fiction." It was the first title in a six-book contract with her new publisher Collins and had an initial print run of 5,500.

Conclusion: Although the characterisation is strong, at times the narrative is rather too dialogue-heavy and the pace is a little woolly. Oddly, Miss Marple's presence is barely felt until the very end – just too late to save the book. **2/5**

2. The Thirteen Problems (1932, ss)

Cases: 'The Tuesday Night Club': A travelling salesman's wife dies one night after eating dinner...

'The Idol House of Astarte': In a lonely Dartmoor grove, a death occurs in a stone summerhouse...

'Ingots of Gold': The search is on for treasure in sunken Spanish ships off the Cornish coast...

'The Bloodstained Pavement': A painting of bloodstains may hold the clue to a wife's drowning...

'Motive vs. Opportunity': A bereaved man leaves all his money to a medium...

'The Thumb Mark of St Peter': A wife's arsenic is apparently unrelated to her husband's death...

'The Blue Geranium': When a wallpaper flower changes colour, an old lady fears for her life...

'The Companion': A woman appears to murder her friend for no apparent reason...

'The Four Suspects': A retired spy is tracked down by a German secret society...

'A Christmas Tragedy': When a wife is murdered at a hydro-hotel, her husband's alibi might not be as watertight as he thinks...

'The Herb of Death': Foxgloves mixed with sage leads to a fatal dose of food poisoning...

'The Affair at the Bungalow': A playwright is accused of robbery after arranging to meet a beautiful actress...

'Death by Drowning': An architect stands accused of murdering an unwed mother-to-be...

Context: The first six stories were written for *Sketch* magazine in 1928, with Christie supplementing them with seven new ones to flesh out the collection. They concern a group of St Mary Mead inhabitants who meet every Tuesday to propound a problem. The group consists of Jane Marple, her nephew Raymond West and his fiancée Joyce Lemprière, ex-commissioner Henry Clithering, clergyman Dr Pender, and the solicitor Mr Petherick.

Conclusion: A pleasing selection of puzzles, each narrated in a different voice. **4/5**

3. The Regatta Mystery (1939*, ss)

Case: 'Miss Marple Tells a Story': Some years before, a young man was charged for his wife's murder in a country hotel...

Context: This is the only Marple story in this mixed collection; it is also the only adventure that she herself narrates. Her nephew Raymond West's wife is here called Joan, despite being established as Joyce in *The Thirteen Problems* (1932).

Conclusion: A good mystery, helped by Miss Marple's own unique narration. **4/5**

4. The Body in the Library (1942)

Case: A young blonde woman is found dead in the library of Miss Marple's friend...

Context: The title for this book – a deliberate cliché of detective fiction – was originally mentioned by Poirot in *Cards on the Table* (1936) as being the work of crime writer Ariadne Oliver. Christie obviously took a shine to the title and thereby further cemented her connection to her fictional counterpart. Christie considered the opening chapter of this book – the first Marple novel for over a decade – as the best she had ever written.

Conclusion: Christie brilliantly turns the clichéd situation on its head in this strong follow-up to the insipid *The Murder at the Vicarage* (1930). **5/5**

5. The Moving Finger (1943)

Case: A series of poison-pen letters causes heartache and suicide in a Devonshire coastal town...

Context: Written during the blackouts of the Second World War, this is one of Christie's favourite works, perhaps because of its wartime romance story. The fictional town of Lymstock appears to be named after the similar Dorset coastal town of Lyme Regis.

Conclusion: A fast-moving narrative and the misdirection of clues is particularly well done. 5/5

6. Three Blind Mice and Other Stories (1950*, ss)

Cases: 'Strange Jest': A practical-joking uncle has died leaving 'hidden treasure'...

'The Tape-Measure Murder': A dressmaker finds her client strangled...

'The Case of the Perfect Maid': A maid is accused of pinching her mistress' brooch...

'The Case of the Caretaker': A doctor's unsolved mystery as the ideal tonic for post 'flu blues...

Context: These stories appeared in British magazines from 1925 to 1942. 'The Case of the Caretaker' anticipates the plot of *Endless Night* (1967) by some years.

Conclusion: 'The Case of the Perfect Maid' is one of Christie's best Marple short stories. 4/5

7. A Murder is Announced (1950)

Case: It's unusual for a murder to be advertised in advance, but that's just what happens one quiet morning in Chipping Cleghorn...

Context: Pushed by Collins as her 50th book [sic], this was the first Christie to reach 50,000 copies on its first print run. Amongst the cosy villagers are an obviously lesbian elderly couple, the first time Christie openly wrote about a female gay relationship.

Conclusion: Although there's a tad too many coincidences for comfort, this is nonetheless a densely plotted mystery with all clues fairly shown. It offers an excellent insight into the changing nature of village life in the aftermath of the Second World War. **4/5**

8. They Do It With Mirrors (1952)

Case: Something is clearly not as it should be in a juvenile reform home...

Context: The book is peppered with Italian insults – unsurprisingly, in Italy these references were toned down. Miss Marple is here described as being in her mid-sixties.

Conclusion: At a time when the world was undergoing huge societal changes, Christie's values were still of the pre-war variety, which unfortunately gives the book a rather dated feel. **2/5**

9. A Pocket Full of Rye (1953)

Case: A handful of grain is found in the pocket of a poisoned businessman...

Context: Christie once again mines the ambiguous stanzas of nursery rhymes for the title of this book (she had used different lines from the same rhyme for two earlier short stories). Unlike some book titles she used, though, the rhyme actually has significance to the plot – people relating to the rhyme are killed off in order. Christie's house at Sunningdale, Berks, was the model for Yewtree Lodge.

Conclusion: Christie on autopilot, but entertaining in its own way. **3/5**

10. 4.50 from Paddington (1957)

Case: A woman witnesses a murder in an adjoining railway carriage...

Context: The title was originally *4.54 from Paddington* before Collins rounded it down at the eleventh hour. But in American editions of the book (entitled *What Mrs McGillicuddy Saw!*), the train keeps its 4.54 departure time. Marple here has a brilliant assistant in the shape of Lucy Eyelesbarrow, but despite her popularity with readers and critics, she never made a repeat appearance.

Conclusion: More tightrope walking to keep the murderer's identity secret, but the tensions of a large family (à la *The Mysterious Affair at Styles*, 1920) are expertly described and the narrative fairly whistles along. **5/5**

11. The Adventure of the Christmas Pudding and a Selection of Entrées (1960†, ss)

Case: 'Greenshaw's Folly': In the grounds of a mansion, a spinster is shot through with an arrow...
Context: This story first appeared in the March 1957 edition of *Ellery Queen's Mystery Magazine*.
Conclusion: The solution to the mystery appears to be plucked from thin air. Unsatisfying. **2/5**

12. Double Sin and Other Stories (1961*, ss)

Cases: 'Greenshaw's Folly': See *The Adventure of the Christmas Pudding* (1960†).
'Sanctuary': In Chipping Cleghorn, a man is found bleeding to death in the church...
Context: This second story had appeared in the October 1954 edition of *Woman's Journal*.
Conclusion: An average tale. **3/5**

13. Thirteen for Luck! (US: 1961, UK: 1966)

'The Blue Geranium': See *The Thirteen Problems* (1932).
'The Four Suspects': Ditto.
'The Tape-Measure Murder': See *Three Blind Mice* (1950*).

14. The Mirror Crack'd from Side to Side (1962)

Case: At a lavish garden fete, one of the guests is fatally poisoned...
Context: The title comes from a line in Alfred Lord Tennyson's poem *The Lady of Shalott* (also quoted in 'Dead Man's Mirror' from *Murder in the Mews*, 1937). The plot is partly based on a tragic occurrence in the life of American actress Gene Tierney – the action switched from Los Angeles to St Mary Mead. The village has changed drastically from its first appearance in *The Murder at the Vicarage* (1930) – servants are fast disappearing, new people are moving in, and a housing development is rising up on nearby pastureland. This was the last time Christie would feature an English village murder mystery in any of her books.
Conclusion: The death-knell of rural England is loudly rung in this clever and satisfying tale of tragedy and revenge, Hollywood-style. **5/5**

15. A Caribbean Mystery (1964)

Case: A retired major is killed whilst holidaying in the Caribbean...

Context: The fictional St Honoré is probably based on St Lucia, a Caribbean island that Christie had visited a few years before writing this book. Apart from her childhood holiday in Italy, this is the only reference to Miss Marple ever leaving her native shores.

Conclusion: One of the best of the latter-day Marples. The West Indian backdrop is convincingly described. **5/5**

16. At Bertram's Hotel (1965)

Case: An old-fashioned hotel is not as reputable as it first seems to be...

Context: Brown's Hotel (est. 1837) on Albermarle Street in Mayfair, London, is used as the model for the fictitious Bertram's Hotel. It was often the refuge for royalty and celebrities, and it is rumoured that Rudyard Kipling wrote *The Jungle Book* (1894) there. Christie herself visited it when she was 14.

Conclusion: The hotel is the star of this curious and slow-moving paean to an earlier, simpler age; the murder seems largely incidental. **2/5**

17. Thirteen Clues for Miss Marple (1966*, ss)

'The Blue Geranium': See *The Thirteen Problems* (1932).

'The Companion': Ditto.

'The Four Suspects': Ditto.

'The Herb of Death': Ditto.

'Motive vs. Opportunity': Ditto.

'The Thumb Mark of St Peter': Ditto.

'The Bloodstained Pavement': Ditto.

'The Case of the Caretaker': See *Three Blind Mice* (1950*).

'The Case of the Perfect Maid': Ditto.

'Strange Jest': Ditto.

'The Tape-Measure Murder': Ditto.

'Greenshaw's Folly': See *The Adventure of the Christmas Pudding* (1960†).

'Sanctuary': See *Double Sin* (1961*)

18. Nemesis (1971)

Case: A message from a dead acquaintance prompts a bus tour to an unknown crime…

Context: This is the last Miss Marple book that Christie wrote. Certain inconsistencies arise due, no doubt, to the author's advancing age

Conclusion: An ambling, repetitious, slow-paced mystery tour of a book, but still quite enjoyable in its own way. **3/5**

19. Sleeping Murder (1976)

Case: The owner of a seaside villa is plagued by strange feelings about its past…

Context: In the early years of the Second World War, Christie wrote final novels for Poirot and Miss Marple and put them into bank vaults, heavily insured against destruction. It was her wish that these books should only be published after her death in order to 'seal' the careers of these two detectives and insure that no poor imitators should come along and resuscitate them. But *Sleeping Murder* is not obviously Marple's last case and it is unclear why it was left until the year of Christie's death to publish it. Certain discrepancies arise because of the age of the manuscript: Colonel Bantry is alive and well (after dying before *The Mirror Crack'd from Side to Side*, 1962), and the lifestyle of the various Dillmouth inhabitants are definitely of the pre-war variety. (Strictly speaking, John Gielgud playing Ferdinand in *The Duchess of Malfi* in London's Theatre Royal fixes the date as 1944.) Christie made over the novel, by deed of gift, to Max Mallowan; in the US, Bantam paid $1m for the paperback rights alone.

Conclusion: This 'blast from the past' would have been considered one of her weaker efforts if published in the 1940s, but compared with her later, much diminished work, it positively glows. **4/5**

20. Miss Marple's Final Cases and Two Other Stories (1979†)

'Miss Marple Tells a Story': See *The Regatta Mystery* (1939*).
'Strange Jest': See *Three Blind Mice* (1950*).
'The Tape-Measure Murder': Ditto.
'The Case of the Caretaker': Ditto.
'The Case of the Perfect Maid': Ditto.
'Sanctuary': See *Double Sin* (1961*).

6

Tommy and Tuppence Beresford

4 novels, 16 short stories

Tommy and Tuppence Beresford

We first meet Thomas Beresford and Prudence Cowley – known to friends as Tommy and Tuppence – just after the First World War, when they are in their 20s (*The Secret Adversary*, 1922). He is an army lieutenant who has seen action in France, Mesopotamia and Egypt, and she is a maid-of-all-work in a London officers' hospital. They meet unexpectedly at Dover Street tube station (now sadly disused) and decide to set themselves up as the 'Young Adventurers, Limited' and advertise in *The Times*: "Two young adventurers for hire. Willing to do anything, go anywhere. Pay must be good. No unreasonable offer refused." Whilst solving their first case they form a strong romantic bond, though they don't confess their true feelings until the villain has been unmasked.

They are always ebullient and enthusiastic, very high-spirited even when in dangerous situations. They love exchanging Wodehousian banter: "Tommy, old thing!" "Tuppence, old bean!" they perpetually cry. And they remain adolescents even into their old age.

After six years of marriage, Tommy is working in the admin department of the Secret Service, and they are both bored with their lot (*Partners in Crime*, 1929). But when the chance comes to run Blunt's International Detective Agency for six months, they jump at it, Tommy claiming he's read every detective novel published in the last decade. At the end of the adventure, Tuppence is pregnant for the first time.

Ten years later and they've got twins – Deborah is in the code-breaking department of British Intelligence while Derek is in the RAF. They must be very bright, as neither can be older than eleven. The Beresfords themselves are too old for active service – he is in his 40s, she is 39 – but the Secret Service asks them off-the-record to hunt down some Fifth Columnists for them, which they throw their heart and soul into (*N or M?*, 1941).

A long time passes before we meet them again. When we do, Tommy is over 70 and Tuppence is 66: "Mr Beresford had once had red hair... but most of it had gone that sandy-cum-grey colour that red-headed people so often arrive at in middle life. Mrs Beresford had once had black hair, a vigorous curling mop of it. Now the black was adulterated with streaks of grey laid on, apparently at random." But they have still not arrived at the time of life "when they thought of themselves as old," and Tuppence finds herself in danger as she tries to uncover the sinister secret of a strange old house (*By the Pricking of My Thumbs*, 1968).

When we last encounter them, they have retired to a new home, The Laurels, in the resort town of Hollowquay. By this time they have three grandchildren, aged 15, 11 and 7. But even in their twilight years they have enough get-up-and-go to investigate a decades-old murder (*Postern of Fate*, 1973).

Albert Batt:

The Beresfords acquired this young Cockney assistant porter during their first adventure, and he goes on to become their lifelong domestic servant. He marries Milly (or Amy) in 1934, at the age of 20, and by 1940 is a publican in Kennington, London. He is 55 in their penultimate case, and when we last see him he is an old man.

Appearances: All.

1. The Secret Adversary (1922)

Case: A shipwreck survivor has documents that could discredit several Tory statesmen...

Context: *The Secret Adversary* was inspired by Christie overhearing a conversation in an ABC teashop about a 'Jane Fish' (changed in the book to 'Jane Finn'). Tommy and Tuppence were modelled on the sort of people who had been demobbed from the armed forces after World War One and were going around selling things door-to-door to make ends meet. Serial rights were sold to *The Weekly Times* and Christie received twice as much as for her first novel. Working titles were *The Joyful Venture* and *The Young Adventurers*.

Conclusion: A bright and airy alternative to Christie's domestic crime stories. **5/5**

2. Partners in Crime (1929)

Cases: 'A Fairy in the Flat': The Beresfords must look out for a letter bearing the number 16...

'A Pot of Tea': A young man wants to trace a missing shop girl...

'The Affair of the Pink Pearl': A precious jewel has been stolen from a titled house guest...

'The Adventure of the Sinister Stranger': Someone is trying to steal a doctor's important research...

'Finessing the King' & 'The Gentleman Dressed in Newspaper': Murder is on the menu at a trendy Bohemian café...

'The Case of the Missing Lady': An arctic explorer seeks his missing fiancée...

'Blindman's Buff': At a smart hotel, a duke asks the Beresfords to help him find his daughter...

'The Man in the Mist': A glamorous actress is being shadowed by a murderer...

'The Crackler': The Beresfords go on the trail of a notorious counterfeiter...

'The Sunningdale Mystery': A man is found stabbed on a golf links...

'The House of Lurking Death': A rich niece receives a box of poisoned chocolates...

'The Unbreakable Alibi': A woman claims she was in two places at once...

'The Clergyman's Daughter' & 'The Red House': A house appears to be 'haunted'...

'The Ambassador's Boots': An ambassador's bag is mysteriously switched with a senator's...

'The Man Who Was No.16': The Beresfords come face to face with their enemy...

Context: The stories in this collection are brilliantly crafted parodies of contemporary fictional detectives – unfortunately, because most of them are nowadays unknown, their impact is considerably lessened. For reasons unknown, Collins also published the last eight stories under the title of *The Sunningdale Mystery* (1929).

Conclusion: Witty, affectionate and impossible to dislike. That Christie has the confidence to spoof her own creations in the final story says as much about her modesty as a writer as it does about her skill as a satirist. **5/5**

3. N or M? (1941)

Case: A group of spies and saboteurs are operating out of a seaside resort...

Context: Christie alternated writing this book with *The Body in the Library* (1942) to keep herself fresh and avoid writer's block. It's the first Christie story to be set during the Second World War.

Conclusion: A rollicking spy adventure, albeit with only a modicum of credibility. **4/5**

4. By the Pricking of My Thumbs (1968)

Case: An old woman in a nursing home speaks of a child being buried behind a fireplace...

Context: The character of Mrs Lancaster and her "Was it your poor child?" query was also used in *The Pale Horse* (1961) and *Sleeping Murder* (1976); it appears to have some personal significance for the author, and perhaps it was based on a real incident.

Conclusion: Surprisingly enjoyable latter-day Christie that keeps you guessing until the end. And although there may be one too many loose ends (or, to be charitable, 'red herrings'), the narrative is always engaging. **4/5**

5. Postern of Fate (1973)

Case: A poisoning many years ago may not have been accidental after all...

Context: The title comes from 'Gates of Damascus', a poem by Lewisham-born poet and playwright James Elroy Flecker (1884–1915). The Laurels is based on Christie's childhood home of Ashfield. The book is generally considered to be Christie's worst (along with *Passenger to Frankfurt*, 1970), and although it made the best-seller charts, the reviews were mostly critical.

Conclusion: A sad end to a good series – an introspective narrative with plenty of dull asides obscures the so-so plot. **1/5**

7

Mr Parker Pyne

14 short stories

Parker Pyne

Plump and bald, Parker Pyne is a retired civil servant in his sixties. He is the son of Charles and Harriet Parker Pyne, and his first name appears to be Christopher, although his bag is marked 'J Parker Pyne'. Wanting to put his 35 year stint compiling statistics for the government to good use, he rents a London office, engages Felicity Lemon as his secretary (who would later work for Hercule Poirot), and places the following advert in *The Times'* personal column: "ARE YOU HAPPY? IF NOT, CONSULT MR PARKER PYNE, 17 RICHMOND STREET." Professing himself more interested in affairs of the heart than grisly murder mysteries (he calls himself a "heart specialist"), he deals almost solely with marital or romantic problems. He often constructs elaborate theatrical charades to fool the suspected parties and always takes an active rôle in solving the various cases. They usually end happily, and because of Pyne's kindly nature, any deceptions committed are soon forgiven.

1. Parker Pyne Investigates (1934)

Cases: 'The Case of the Middle-Aged Wife': A wife must find a way to make her husband jealous…
'The Case of the Discontented Soldier': A retired major finds himself in the thick of action again…
'The Case of the Distressed Lady': A diamond needs to returned to its owner before she notices…
'The Case of the Discontented Husband': A man struggles to regain the love of his wife before she leaves him…
'The Case of the City Clerk': A mild-mannered clerk seeks a new life of excitement and romance…
'The Case of the Rich Woman': A lonely woman decides she wants a different circle of friends…

'Have You Got Everything You Want?': On the Simplon-Orient Express, a wife thinks her husband is plotting against her...

'The Gate of Baghdad': An RAF officer dies in the desert before he can reveal the truth about a mysterious disappearance...

'The House at Shiraz': A German pilot has fallen in love with an eccentric English recluse...

'The Pearl of Price': A woman's valuable pearl is stolen and her travelling companions are suspected...

'Death on the Nile': On a Nile charter boat, a wife thinks her husband is trying to poison her...

'The Oracle at Delphi': Greek bandits kidnap a woman's son in return for her jewel necklace...

Context: The first six cases (written for magazines in 1932) take place in London under Parker Pyne's auspices as a detective, while the following six show him on holiday and acting as reluctant adviser or investigator in various exotic locales. Christie used these locations to greater effect in some of her later novels, such as *Murder on the Orient Express* (1934) and *Death on the Nile* (1937), the latter even sharing its name with the penultimate short story.

Conclusion: A charming collection of romantically inclined mysteries. **4/5**

2. The Regatta Mystery (1939*)

Cases: 'The Regatta Mystery': A diamond disappears in front of a roomful of party guests...

'Problem at Pollensa Bay': A mother is worried about her son's affair with a young artist...

Context: These are the only two Parker Pyne stories not included in the first collection, *Parker Pyne Investigates*.

Conclusion: Two clever tales. **4/5**

3. Poirot Lends a Hand (1946)

'The Regatta Mystery': See *The Regatta Mystery* (1939*).
'Problem at Pollensa Bay': Ditto.

4. Problem at Pollensa Bay (1991†)

'The Regatta Mystery': See *The Regatta Mystery* (1939*).
'Problem at Pollensa Bay': Ditto.

8

Mr Harley Quin

14 short stories

Harley Quin

Harley Quin is a mystery. He appears and disappears unexpectedly, and by strange tricks of light caused by stained-glass windows or flickering firelight his clothes often seem bright and multicoloured, like the theatrical Harlequin figure. His background, family and friends are unknown and his seemingly supernatural powers offer a stark contrast to the earnest rationality of Poirot or Marple.

Quin helps his friend Mr Satterthwaite in solving the various puzzles they encounter, not by direct action, but more by a process of helpful prodding. He is merely the catalyst; he appears from nowhere asking a few pertinent questions, and focuses Satterthwaite's mind on the correct solution. He reminds his friend of what he *actually* saw and heard, rather than what he *assumed* he saw and heard, and once enlightened, the solution is usually within Satterthwaite's grasp.

Mr Satterthwaite

Because Harley Quin is such an enigmatic figure, Satterthwaite is the normal man who counteracts his behaviour and interprets his actions for the aid of the reader. He is, in essence, a snob who combines his hobbies as art connoisseur and amateur photographer with the carefree lifestyle of a bachelor. But underlying this freedom is a deep vein of loneliness; he spends his life observing other people and trying to see what makes them tick.

1. The Mysterious Mr Quin (1930)

Cases: 'The Coming of Mr Quin': A mysterious stranger appears on New Year's Eve...

'The Shadow on the Glass': The return of an old flame has alarming consequences...

'At the Bells and Motley': A woman's fiancé is being framed for murder...

'The Sign in the Sky': Train smoke turns a murder case on its head...

'The Soul of the Croupier': A love triangle in Monte Carlo leads to danger...

'The World's End': A valuable opal goes missing on Corsica...

'The Voice in the Dark': A drowned woman appears to be haunting her family seat...

'The Face of Helen': Two men struggle for the love of a frightened girl...

'The Dead Harlequin': An artist implicates Quin in an old murder...

'The Bird with the Broken Wing': A séance predicts a murder...

'The Man from the Sea': In the Mediterranean, an unhappy man is attempting suicide...

'Harlequin's Lane': An innocent harlequinade has an unforeseen effect on a family...

Context: As a young girl Christie had become fascinated with the cast of stock characters that populated the commedia dell'arte, an improvised popular comedy that began in Italy in the 16th century. Columbine, Pierrot, Pierette, Punchinello, Punchinella and, most famously, Harlequin, clowned around to entertain the public – the latter, with his bright, multicoloured costume, was her favourite. The eighteenth century Anglicised version of the harlequinade transformed Harlequin from a faithful valet to a romantic figure (usually paired with Columbine), and his ability to make himself invisible at key moments added to his mystery. This is a collection of stories first published in various magazines in the 1920s but despite Christie citing Harley Quin as one of her favourite characters, he rarely makes another appearance.

Conclusion: Apart from two isolated cases, this is all we get to see of the mysterious Harley Quin. Perhaps Christie thought she couldn't maintain the mystery if he became a regularly returning character, so we must be thankful we have these superbly-crafted little tales to remind ourselves just how diverse Christie's talent was. **5/5**

2. Three Blind Mice and Other Stories (1950*)

Case: 'The Love Detectives': A messy love triangle leads to murder...
Context: The single Harley Quin tale in this collection was written in the 1920s but for some reason not included in the original 1930 collection.

Conclusion: A welcome return for the mysterious Quin. **4/5**

3. Problem at Pollensa Bay and Other Stories (1991†)

Cases: 'The Love Detectives': See *Three Blind Mice* (1950*)
'The Harlequin Tea Set': Satterthwaite once more seeks inspiration from his enigmatic friend...
Context: The second Quin story in this miscellaneous collection had previously seen print in *Winter's Crimes 3* (1971) and *Ellery Queen's Murdercade* (1975).
Conclusion: Not as effective as Quin's earlier outings; some of the mystery is missing by now. **3/5**

4. The Harlequin Tea Set (1997*)

'The Harlequin Tea Set': See *Problem At Pollensa Bay* (1991†)

9

Miscellaneous Thrillers

6 novels

Christie peppered her output of detective stories with what she referred to as "light-hearted thrillers". Written in a deliberately up-tempo style and laced with international plots, secret weapons and clandestine organisations, they are a far cry from her Poirot and Marple mysteries – though they often have a strong 'whodunit' element.

1. The Man in the Brown Suit (1924)

Case: A young woman investigates an 'accidental' death at a tube station...

Context: The larger-than-life character of Sir Eustace Pedler was based on Christie's brash friend Major Ernest R Belcher. The working title was *Murder at Mill House*, a reference to Belcher's own house at Dorney, Bucks. Christie was paid £500 for a serialisation in the London *Evening News*, with the title, much to her chagrin, changed to *Anna the Adventuress*; she bought her first car, a Morris Cowley, with the money.

Conclusion: A fast-paced melodrama with plenty of good scenes and more than a few clever twists. **4/5**

2. The Secret of Chimneys (1925)

Case: A young drifter finds diplomatic intrigue, blackmail and murder at an English country house...

Context: This is the last of Christie's books to be published by The Bodley Head. 'The Blitz' hotel is obviously based on The Ritz (although oddly resited to the location of The Savoy), while the machinations of 'Herzoslovakia' owe more than a passing debt to Anthony Hope's *The Prisoner of Zenda* (1894).

Conclusion: A PG Wodehousian comedy-adventure that's a little too slight for its own good. **3/5**

3. The Seven Dials Mystery (1929)

Case: A healthy young man dies in his sleep despite the ringing of eight alarm clocks...

Context: Written as a direct sequel to *The Secret of Chimneys* (1925), the action once again takes place at the titular stately home with many of the same characters returning.

Conclusion: With its reliance on 'jolly hockey sticks' humour, familiar characters and settings, and bumbling upper class twits, this is more like PG Wodehouse than ever. There are many unrewarding dialogue scenes between the loosely connected set-pieces. **2/5**

4. They Came to Baghdad (1951)

Case: A lovesick young girl becomes embroiled in a plot to destroy world peace...

Context: Since 1928 Christie had visited Baghdad many times on her archaeological trips with her husband Max Mallowan – they had a house overlooking the river Tigris – and so the setting was therefore a very familiar one for this, her first thriller for a decade. In Chapter 3 there is an in-joke about fellow thriller writer Edgar Wallace's novel *Sanders of the River* (1911).

Conclusion: Preposterous shenanigans take place in a wholly believable locale – an oddly disjointed mix, but quite readable. **3/5**

5. Destination Unknown (1954)

Case: A security agent goes on the trail of a missing atomic scientist...

Context: The plot is based on two 1950s physicists who betrayed their countries: Bruno Pontecorvo worked for Canada, America and England before defecting to the Soviet Union in 1950, and Emil Fuchs, who was head of theoretical physics at Harwell in England, arrested the same year for spying for the Russians.

Conclusion: Compared to the cynical realism of Ian Fleming (*Casino Royale* was published a year earlier), this frothy pre-war fantasy was rather dated even by 1950s standards. **2/5**

6. Passenger to Frankfurt (1970)

Case: A middle-aged diplomat struggles against a fascist society bent on world domination...

Context: Written in six weeks and published to coincide with her eightieth birthday (subtitled 'An Extravaganza'), Collins printed the largest amount yet of a first edition – 58,000 copies. The book is generally considered her worst (along with *Postern of Fate*, 1973) but despite universally unfavourable reviews, the book sold extremely well.

Conclusion: A muddled, incomprehensible jumble of situations and characters with little – other than the author's rants against permissive society – to link them. But after a while the sheer weirdness of the book draws you in. **3/5**

10

Miscellaneous Mysteries

10 novels, 18 short stories

As well as her thriller stories, Christie also wrote several mysteries that excluded her more famous detectives. These range in style from the PG Wodehouse antics of *Why Didn't They Ask Evans* (1934) to the brooding menace of *Endless Night* (1967) and cover some of her most popular – and most dramatised – stories.

1. The Sittaford Mystery (1931)

Case: A séance in a snowbound Dartmoor house leads to murder…
Context: This is the first time Christie touched on a supernatural theme in one of her novels. The fictional village of Sittaford is located on Bridestowe and Sourton Common, Dartmoor, close to her hometown of Torquay. (The real Sittaford Tor is situated five miles south-east.) Elements of the plot are similar to the later short story 'Three Blind Mice' (from the 1950 collection), the basis for the stage play *The Mousetrap* (1952).
Conclusion: A confident, atmospheric mystery story with more than a hint of *The Hound of the Baskervilles.* **4/5**

2. The Hound of Death and Other Stories (1933†, ss)

Case: 'The Witness for the Prosecution': A husband is framed for murdering an old lady…
Context: The only crime story in this supernaturally orientated collection, it is one of Christie's most famous works – she later adapted it for the stage in 1953 (altering its ending) and it was filmed by Billy Wilder in 1957.
Conclusion: This is a great story told with economy and style – and what a brilliant twist…**5/5**

3. The Listerdale Mystery (1934†, ss)

Cases: 'The Listerdale Mystery': A cheap town-house seems to have a shady past...

'Philomel Cottage': The arrival of an old flame produces grim nightmares...

'The Girl in the Train': A young playboy hides a girl in his train carriage...

'Sing a Song of Sixpence': An eccentric wealthy aunt is murdered...

'The Manhood of Edward Robinson': A mild-mannered shop clerk wins a fortune...

'Accident': A retired inspector suspects a woman to be a dangerous husband killer...

'Jane in Search of a Job': A girl is asked to impersonate a duchess...

'A Fruitful Sunday': A young couple finds something exciting in a basket of cherries...

'Mr Eastwood's Adventure': A mystery writer is arrested for murder...

'The Golden Ball': A disowned nephew's offer of marriage leads to trouble...

'The Rajah's Emerald': A cuckolded clerk stumbles across a valuable jewel...

'Swan Song': A soprano seeks revenge at a charity performance...

Context: A selection of mysteries, most of them light-hearted and some of them romantically inclined, that appeared in America in various different collections over the years.

Conclusion: The strongest collection of Christie's non-detective short stories, the best two here being 'Philomel Cottage' and 'Accident'. **5/5**

4. Why Didn't They Ask Evans? (1934)

Case: When a man plunges down a cliff, two adventurous friends decide to find his killer...

Context: The first of five Christie books published in 1934, it features characters similar to Tommy and Tuppence Beresford. A car crash deception midway through is echoed in Poirot's *Three Act Tragedy* (1935). It is a moot point whether its American title, *The Boomerang Clue*, gives away the ending.

Conclusion: Bright, witty, genuinely funny, this is as close to the perfect light-hearted murder mystery as Christie ever came. **5/5**

5. Murder is Easy (1939)

Case: On her way to Scotland Yard to report a series of murders, an old woman is knocked down by a hit-and-run driver...

Context: This is one of the few Christie stories to feature a homosexual, in this case a Mr Ellsworthy (who has a "mincing walk"). The 'detective' is a young policeman who investigates the murders out of curiosity.

Conclusion: Eclipsed by her more famous offerings in this period, this is a strong Miss Marple-type story that has all the quintessential Christie trademarks. **4/5**

6. Ten Little Niggers (1939)

Case: On an isolated private island, ten invited guests are bumped off one by one...

Context: The title comes from an 1869 English minstrel show song written by Frank Green, based on an American version called *Ten Little Indians* written the year before by Septimus Winner. Christie adopted Green's downbeat ending for the book, and Winner's happy one for her later stage version. Considered racially offensive, the title was changed in America to *And Then There Were None* (it also appeared there as *Ten Little Indians* and *The Nursery Rhyme Murders*). On its English stage revival in 1966, protest groups forced a title change to *And Then There Were None*, and the novel followed suit from 1984. In all cases, the relevant text was altered accordingly. Nigger/Indian Island was apparently based on Burgh Island, off the Devonshire coastal town of Bigbury-on-Sea.

Conclusion: Sinister location, archetypal characters, plotting to die for – what more could you want? **5/5**

7. Towards Zero (1944)

Case: At a clifftop seaside house, an elderly widow is murdered...

Context: Similar in theme to the short story 'The Man from the Sea' (*The Mysterious Mr Quin*, 1930), various Devonshire localities appear in the book – the Yealm River is the 'River Tern', Salcombe is 'Saltcreek', the town of Kingsbridge with its estuary features as 'Saltington' and Bolt Head becomes 'Stark Head'. It features the last appearance of Superintendent Battle.

Conclusion: Despite strong characterisation, the murder occurs too late to energise the narrative. **2/5**

8. Death Comes as the End (1945)

Case: An Egyptian priest's concubine dies in mysterious circumstances...

Context: Christie's only attempt at historical fiction, its genesis came from a suggestion by noted Egyptologist Stephen RK Glanville that she should write a murder mystery set in ancient Egypt. She used as reference some XI Dynasty letters that the New York Metropolitan Museum of Art had unearthed in the 1920s, combined with historical details gleaned by Glanville himself. He suggested – and Christie agreed – that the ending should be altered, something that the author would later regret.

Conclusion: Christie spends more effort in recreating the historical background than on the complexities of the plot – but it's worth reading as a failed experiment. **3/5**

9. Sparkling Cyanide (1945)

Cast: A beautiful heiress is fatally poisoned in a West End restaurant...

Context: This 'murder in retrospect' novel is based on the short story 'Yellow Iris' (*The Regatta Mystery*, 1939*); it was the first title to reach sales of 30,000 copies in its first year of publication. Colonel Johnny Race, now in his sixties, makes his final appearance.

Conclusion: An average Christie, but still readable. **3/5**

10. The Witness for the Prosecution (1948*, ss)

'The Witness for the Prosecution': See *The Hound of Death* (1933†).
'Philomel Cottage': See *The Listerdale Mystery* (1934 †).
'Accident': Ditto.
'Sing a Song of Sixpence': Ditto.

11. Crooked House (1949)

Case: A wealthy Greek businessman is found dead in his London home...

Context: Christie often said this was one of her favourite detective novels. The crooked house in question (like many of her titles, a reference to a nursery rhyme) was based on Christie's old home of Scotswood in Sunningdale, Berks.

Conclusion: The ending impresses in this otherwise rather patchy read. **3/5**

12. Three Blind Mice and Other Stories (1950*, ss)

Case: 'Three Blind Mice': Residents of a guesthouse are trapped by a snowstorm and stalked by a killer...

Context: This short story was originally written as a thirty minute radio play to celebrate the eightieth birthday of Queen Mary, mother of King George VI: it was broadcast on 26 May 1947. As well as later working it into prose form, Christie also staged it for the theatre, changing its name to *The Mousetrap* (1952). Christie asked for the story to be withheld from publication in her native country until the London theatrical run concluded. With no sign of this ever happening, HarperCollins finally published it in 2012 in the UK.

Conclusion: The derivative set-up works better on the stage than the page. **2/5**

13. Ordeal by Innocence (1958)

Case: A boy is falsely accused of killing his adopted mother...

Context: The fictional Sunny Point house is based on Christie's own home of Greenway in Devon (both were used as children's refuges in World War Two). It overlooks the river Dart, which becomes the river 'Rubicon' in the novel. Christie always maintained that this and *Crooked House* (1949) were her most satisfying books.

Conclusion: Amnesia is always a cop-out, and it's hard to know why this book is one of Christie's personal favourites (unless it ties in with her 1926 disappearance). But it has its moments. **3/5**

14. Surprise! Surprise! (1965*, ss)

'The Mystery of the Spanish Shawl': The alternative title for 'Mr Eastwood's Adventure' – see *The Listerdale Mystery* (1934†).

'The Witness for the Prosecution': See *The Witness for the Prosecution* (1948*).

15. Endless Night (1967)

Case: A working class man buys a piece of land that appears to be cursed...

Context: More a suspense story than a conventional mystery, it was inspired by an area of land on Welsh moorland called Gipsy's Acre. The title comes from William Blake's poem 'Auguries of Innocence'.

Conclusion: This is another excellent late Christie, with convincing characterisation (especially that of the psychotic killer) and atmosphere you could cut with a knife. **5/5**

16. The Golden Ball and Other Stories (1971*, ss)

'The Listerdale Mystery': See *The Listerdale Mystery* (1934)
'The Girl in the Train': Ditto.
'The Manhood of Edward Robinson': Ditto.
'A Fruitful Sunday': Ditto.
'The Golden Ball': Ditto.
'The Rajah's Emerald': Ditto.
'Swan Song': Ditto.

17. While the Light Lasts (1997†, ss)

Cases: 'The Actress': A woman deals with her blackmailer...
'The Edge': Revenge does not always go to plan...
'Manx Gold': Thrills and spills on an Isle of Man treasure hunt...
'Within a Wall': A tragic love triangle has far-reaching consequences...
Context: These four early short stories appeared in various publications in 1930. 'Manx Gold' was a glorified set of clues for a car treasure hunt competition, run by the Isle of Man Tourist Board.
Conclusion: Bar 'The Actress', a very weak selection. **2/5**

18. The Harlequin Tea Set (1997*, ss)

'The Actress': See *While the Light Lasts* (1997†).
'The Edge': Ditto.
'Manx Gold': Ditto.
'Within a Wall': Ditto.

11

Collaborative Mysteries

4 chapters

The following two books feature Christie's brief involvement in co-writing stories with fellow authors.

1. The Floating Admiral (1931)

Case: At a seaside holiday resort, an admiral's corpse is discovered floating down the river...

Context: Christie provided the fourth chapter of this book, whose twelve segments were written separately by members of the Detection Club of London, a private club of mystery writers formed in 1928 by Dorothy L Sayers and Anthony Berkeley. (Christie became the club's Co-President in 1958, a position she held until her death in 1976.) Rules stipulated that the authors should structure their chapters such that a realistic solution could be arrived at – in other words, they shouldn't deliberately complicate matters to hinder later writers. Other contributors included GK Chesterton, Freeman Wills Croft and Dorothy L Sayers.

Conclusion: Amazingly, the story steers along very well despite the many different hands at the tiller. Christie's solution is typically ingenuous, but ultimately comes to naught. **4/5**

2. The Scoop and Behind The Screen (1983)

Cases: 'Behind the Screen': A house guest is found murdered behind a large Japanese screen...

'The Scoop': A newspaper reporter is killed while covering a murder case...

Context: These are the texts of two BBC radio series, the first broadcast from June to July 1930 in six parts, the second from January to March 1931 in twelve parts. Christie wrote the second episode of *Behind the Screen*, and the second and fourth episodes of *The Scoop* and, like the other contributors (including Dorothy L Sayers, Hugh Walpole, Ronald Knox and Freeman Wills Croft), she read them live on air.

Conclusion: A forerunner to *The Floating Admiral*, these two stories betray their aural roots a little too obviously and the plotting is inconsistent. 3/5

12

The Supernatural

1 novel, 14 short stories

Christie was always fascinated by supernatural themes and some of her earliest fiction (indeed, her very first story) concentrates on the occult as much as it does on crime. In these often scary tales she allows herself the luxury of creating fear and suspense through her imaginative descriptive powers – something she would limit in her mainstream mystery and thriller books.

1. The Hound of Death and Other Stories (1933†, ss)

Cases: 'The Hound of Death': A nun blows up her convent by psychic powers...

'The Red Signal': A séance predicts bloody death...

'The Fourth Man': A mentally disabled Brittany peasant has developed multiple personalities...

'The Gipsy': A man has visions of a gypsy with a red scarf...

'The Lamp': In a haunted house, a boy discovers an invisible playmate...

'Wireless': A dead husband communicates to his wife through a newly bought radio...

'The Mystery of the Blue Jar': A golfer keeps hearing a cry of "Murder!"...

'The Strange Case of Sir Arthur Carmichael': An heir to a title starts behaving like a cat...

'The Call of Wings': Hypnotic street music draws a man into the spiritual realms...

'The Last Séance': Weird things happen during a medium's final appearance...

'SOS': A scrawled message leads to a puzzle about a family's inheritance...

Context: The stories in this collection appear to hail from a very early period in Christie's life, possibly predating her first published novel, *The Mysterious Affair at Styles*, in 1920. Although not published in

America, the individual stories have been anthologised in other Christie collections.

Conclusion: An interesting collection of Christie juvenilia, notable for her rare abandonment of the crime/thriller genre. Most of the tales are frightening and suspenseful, and although at times they can be overwritten, there is no doubting their effectiveness. **4/5**

2. The Regatta Mystery (1939*, ss)

Case: 'In a Glass Darkly': A house guest is shocked to see a future murder reflected in his bedroom mirror...

Context: The only ghost story in this collection, it would have fitted far more comfortably into the earlier collection of supernatural tales, replacing perhaps 'Witness for the Prosecution'.

Conclusion: Undoubtedly chilling. **4/5**

3. The Witness for the Prosecution (1948*, ss)

'The Red Signal': See *The Hound of Death* (1933†).
'The Fourth Man': Ditto.
'SOS': Ditto.
'Where There's a Will': Ditto (under its original title of 'Wireless').
'The Mystery of the Blue Jar': Ditto.

4. Double Sin and Other Stories (1961*, ss)

Cases: 'The Dressmaker's Doll': A velvet-suited toy appears to possess some rather sinister qualities...

'The Last Séance': See *The Hound of Death* (1933†).

Context: An American collection of stories ranging from the 1920s to the 1950s.

Conclusion: This single new horror story is effectively open-ended. **4/5**

5. The Pale Horse (1961)

Case: A priest's death leads to sinister goings on in an old country inn...

Context: The idea for this book came from Christie's experiences on a pharmaceutical course she took in her youth, specifically the strange activities of its tutor, a 'Mr P'. She described thallium poisoning so accurately that in 1975 a nurse recognised the symptoms after reading the book and was able to save a man from being poisoned by his wife. A similar case followed in 1977 when a nurse saved the life of a 19–month-old baby. But by far the most famous proponent of thallium as a poison was Graham Young, known as 'The St Albans Poisoner'. He got a job serving as a lab assistant at a photographic company in Bovingdon, Herts, and there attempted to poison the other workers, successfully killing two of them. He was arrested in 1971, and his life story was immortalised in the 1995 film *The Young Poisoner's Handbook*. Ariadne Oliver appears without Poirot here, the only time she does so in a novel. The title is a Bible quotation from Revelation 6:8.

Conclusion: One of Christie's darkest efforts, blending witchcraft, secret societies and murder to great effect. **4/5**

6. The Golden Ball and Other Stories (1971*, ss)

'The Hound of Death: See *The Hound of Death* (1933†).
'The Gipsy': Ditto.
'The Lamp': Ditto.
'The Strange Case of Sir Arthur Carmichael': Ditto.
'The Call of Wings': Ditto.

7. Miss Marple's Final Cases and Two Other Stories (1979, ss)

'In a Glass Darkly': See *The Regatta Mystery* (1939†).
'The Dressmaker's Doll': See *Double Sin* (1961*).

8. While the Light Lasts (1997†, ss)

Case: 'The House of Dreams': The search for a perfect home blurs the boundaries between dreams and reality…
Context: This is a reworked version of Christie's very first short story, written in 1908 and originally entitled 'The House of Beauty'.
Verdict: Probably the worst written of her stories, it is interesting only as an example of Christie's juvenilia. **1/5**

9. The Harlequin Tea Set (1997*, ss)

'The House of Dreams': See *While the Light Lasts* (1997†).

13

Romances

6 novels, 4 short stories

During Christie's long literary career she produced a handful of stories that were not concerned with crime or its consequences, but with relationships between family, friends and lovers – for want of a better word, 'romances'. Nowadays this is usually a derogatory term for sentimentalised women's fiction, but Christie's romances had more in common with Daphne du Maurier than Mills & Boon. Her publisher, Collins, disliked these offerings, feeling it was being cheated out of 'proper' crime books, but were obliged to publish them (albeit under the pseudonym of Mary Westmacott) in order to keep their bestselling author happy. Her real identity was revealed in 1949.

1. Giant's Bread (1930)

Story: When a gifted composer returns home after being reported killed in the war, he finds his wife has already remarried…

Observations: Based on the short story 'While the Light Lasts' (from *While the Light Lasts*, 1997†), the character of the composer, Vernon Deyre, may well have been based on teenage pianist and composer Roger Sacheverell Coke, a friend of Christie's sister. The novel was twice as long as Christie's detective stories and the initial reviews were quietly encouraging.

Verdict: A gripping narrative about the human condition, with sentiment eschewed in favour of rigorous soul-searching. A tad long perhaps, but still remarkably coherent. **5/5**

2. Unfinished Portrait (1934)

Story: A female novelist attempts suicide after a marriage break-up…

Observations: Christie's most autobiographical venture into fiction, the book shed much-needed light on her 1926 disappearance, following her break-up with her first husband Archie. The fictional novelist Celia is clearly a thinly disguised version of the author, and many incidents in the novel (such as Celia's memories of childhood) are ones that Christie herself experienced.

Verdict: Great as autobiography, not so good as fiction, here we get as close to Christie the person as we ever will. **4/5**

3. Absent in the Spring (1944)

Story: A middle-aged woman tries to come to terms with her husband's love for another woman...

Observations: The title is a quotation from a Shakespearian sonnet. The 50,000 word novel was written in three days, including a 'sick day' from the dispensary she worked in at University College Hospital.

Verdict: The clinically analytical tone is undoubtedly impressive, and the subject is clearly close to Christie's heart, but there's something rather detached about the narrative that makes it hard to empathise with the central character. **3/5**

4. The Rose and the Yew Tree (1947)

Story: A working class man's attempts to elevate himself in life lead to unforeseen consequences...

Observations: The title derives from the last poem in TS Eliot's *Four Quarters* (1944), 'Little Giddings': "The moment of the rose and the moment of the yew-tree are of equal duration."

Verdict: An introspective, rather cynical, novel that internalises most of its plot and offers little by way of comfort. **2/5**

5. A Daughter's a Daughter (UK: 1952, US: 1963)

Story: A mother rejects personal happiness to look after her daughter, but later regrets her decision...

Observations: Five years after her last Westmacott book, Christie produced this story about a love-hate relationship between mother and daughter, which appears to be the least autobiographical of all her romances. It was based on a 1930s play, unperformed until 1956.

Verdict: A generally effective tale about self-destructive mother-love told with conviction and honesty. **4/5**

6. The Burden (UK: 1956, US: 1963)

Story: In controlling the life of her younger sibling, a girl precipitates a disastrous marriage…

Observations: This last novel Christie wrote as Mary Westmacott uses themes already explored in her previous book, but laced with an existentialist slant courtesy of 'Dr Llewellyn Knox', an American evangelist seemingly based on the real-life preacher Billy Graham.

Verdict: This reads like a reworking of her previous Westmacott story, which dampens the effect. **2/5**

7. The Golden Ball and Other Stories (1971*, ss)

Stories: 'Magnolia Blossom': A wife has second thoughts about leaving her bankrupted husband…

'Next to a Dog: A poor widow considers an unpleasant marriage in order to care for her dog…

Observations: These two romance stories probably date from the 1920s.

Verdict: Sentimental and contrived, especially the latter story with its grotesquely literal puppy love. **2/5**

8. Problem at Pollensa Bay (1991†, ss)

'Magnolia Blossom': See *The Golden Ball* (1971*).
'Next to a Dog': Ditto.

9. While the Light Lasts (1997†, ss)

Stories: 'The Lonely God': A man and woman meet in a museum and begin to fall in love…

'While the Light Lasts': A husband returns from the war to find his wife in the arms of another…

Observations: The first story appeared in *Royal* magazine of 1926; Christie later said it was "regrettably sentimental". The second one was originally printed in a 1924 issue of the magazine *Novel* and a few years later provided the plot for *Giant's Bread* (1930).

Verdict: Again, two slight and over-sentimental stories. **2/5**

10. The Harlequin Tea Set (1997*)

'The Lonely God': See *While the Light Lasts* (1997†).
'While the Light Lasts': Ditto.

14

Poems and Children's Stories

3 collections

1. The Road of Dreams (1924)

Observations: This was published by Geoffrey Bles and divided into four sections: 'A Masque from Italy' (concerning commedia dell'arte characters), 'Ballads', 'Dreams and Fantasies' and 'Other Poems'. The various poems were written over a twenty-year period.
Verdict: Overtly sentimental. **2/5**

2. Star Over Bethlehem and Other Stories (1965)

Observations: Writing as Agatha Christie Mallowan, this slim volume (79 pages) is made up of six stories and five poems, and was marketed as a children's book for Christmas.
Verdict: The overall theme is one of religious piety of a rather old-fashioned kind. **3/5**

3. Poems (1973)

Observations: A collection of 62 poems, Volume I is a slightly amended reprint of *The Road of Dreams* (1924) while Volume II is new (apart from one poem from *Star Over Bethlehem*) – its four sections are entitled 'Things', 'Places', 'Love Poems and Others' and 'Verses of Nowadays'.
Verdict: Nothing much of interest here – Christie was always a better storyteller than a poet. **2/5**

15

Memoirs

2 volumes

A private person, Christie's two autobiographical works offer highly selective glimpses into her childhood and her archaeological experiences. She hardly touches on her career as a bestselling novelist, instead concentrating on incidents and people that amused her, usually from the early part of her life.

1. Come, Tell Me How You Live (1946)

Observations: An account of Christie's Middle Eastern archaeological digs in the 1930s with Max Mallowan. Her publisher, Collins, disliked the book and, partly due to paper shortages, only produced a small print run of the first edition. To distance it from her crime output, Christie added 'Mallowan' to her name, as she did with some of her romantic fiction. The title is a pun – 'tell' is Arabic for a mound or hill formed by a buried archaeological site.

Verdict: Written in the present tense (a style that seems years ahead of its time), this is a charming, frothy, eminently readable account of what was obviously a very happy period for the author. 5/5

2. An Autobiography (1977)

Observations: Started on 2 April 1950 in a mud-brick house in Nimrud, Iraq and completed fifteen years later at Winterbrook House in Oxfordshire, this "lucky dip" of memories was withheld from publication until after Christie's death, and was revised and edited by her daughter Rosalind Hicks.

Verdict: Frustratingly there is no mention of her 1926 disappearance and not a great deal about her tremendous literary career – most of the book is taken up with childhood memories, wartime stories and family anecdotes. Undoubtedly interesting, but one longs for a weightier self-analysis. 3/5

16

Stage Plays

17 plays

For reasons of space, American casts and details (where relevant) have been excluded. Unless otherwise stated, premieres are in the UK.

1. Black Coffee (1930)

Cast: Francis L Sullivan (Poirot), John Boxer, Richard Fisher, Josephine Middleton, Joyce Bland, Lawrence Hardman, Judith Mentrath, Andre Van Gyseghem, Wallace Evennett, Donald Wolfit, Walter Tennyson
Crew: Director Andre Van Gyseghem
Premiere: 8 December 1930.
Observations: This is the first time Christie wrote an original theatre script; after try-outs at the Embassy Theatre in Swiss Cottage, the play switched to the West End in 1931 for several months (at the St Martin's Theatre, famous for the perennial *The Mousetrap*). It was novelised by Charles Osborne in 1998.
Verdict: A 'missing formula' thriller that lends itself to the stage. **4/5**

2. Akhnaton (circa 1937)

Observations: This was an unperformed Christie play set in Ancient Egypt that foreshadowed her later historical novel *Death Comes as the End* (1945). The script was finally published by Collins in 1973. It has only been seen in repertory or amateur productions.
Verdict: A fascinating polemic on anti-appeasement; perhaps a little dry but otherwise of much interest. **4/5**

3. Ten Little Niggers (1943)

Cast: William Murray, Hilda Bruce-Potter, Reginald Barlow, Linden Travers, Terence de Marney, Michael Blake, Percy Walsh, Eric Cowley, Henrietta Watson

Crew: Director Irene Hentschel
Premieres: 29 September 1943 (UK), 27 June 1944 (US).
Observations: This marked the first time that Christie adapted one of her own books for the stage (in this case the 1939 novel of the same name). It proved to be a great success, with the title changed to the less offensive *Ten Little Indians* for its American run (and also in the UK from 1966). A musical comedy called *Something's Afoot* (1976) was a thinly disguised send-up.
Verdict: The novel transfers well to the stage, despite the unnecessary up-beat ending. **4/5**

4. Appointment with Death (1945)

Cast: Percy Walsh, Mary Clare, Dern Kerbey, Ian Lubbock, John Wynn, Beryl Machin, Janet Burnell, Joan Hickson, Gerard Hinze, Carla Lehmann
Crew: Director Terence de Marney
Premiere: 31 March 1945.
Observations: Christie altered many of the details of her 1938 novel, most significantly changing the identity of the murderer and entirely deleting Poirot. Joan Hickson (the definitive Miss Marple) here makes her second appearance in a Christie adaptation, the first being the 1937 film *Love from a Stranger*.
Verdict: Obvious humour pads out a dialogue-heavy production. **3/5**

5. Murder on the Nile (1945)

Cast: James Roberts, Helen Hayes, Joanna Derill, Ronald Millar, Jacqueline Robert, Hugo Schuster, Ivan Brandt, Rosemary Scott, David Horne
Crew: Director Claude Guerney
Premiere: 9 April 1945 (UK), 19 September 1946 (US).
Observations: Poirot is again scrapped, this time in Christie's adaptation of *Death on the Nile* (1937). The title change is mysterious (the working title was *Moon on the Nile*), and the American one – *Hidden Horizon* – even more so. This stateside version was a flop, only managing twelve performances.
Verdict: The book's lush scenery is sorely missed. **2/5**

6. The Hollow (1951)

Cast: Beryl Baxter, George Thorpe, Jeanne de Casalis, Jessica Spencer, AJ Brown, Colin Douglas, Patricia Jones, Joan Newell, Ernest Clark, Shaw Taylor
Crew: Director Hubert Gregg
Premiere: 5 February 1951.
Observations: Poirot was again missing from this version of Christie's 1946 novel, a bland Scotland Yard detective taking his place. After transferring from Cambridge, the play ran for almost a year in London.
Verdict: A lively adaptation of one of Christie's lesser-known works. 4/5

7. The Mousetrap (1952)

Cast: Richard Attenborough, Sheila Sim, John Paul, Allan McClelland, Mignon O'Doherty, Aubrey Dexter, Jessica Spencer, Martin Miller
Crew: Director Peter Cotes
Premieres: 6 October 1952 (UK), 5 November 1960 (US).
Observations: In 1951 Christie decided to use the short story 'Three Blind Mice' (from *Three Blind Mice*, 1950*), itself a prose version of a 1947 radio play, as the basis for a new theatre presentation (mixed, perhaps, with the setting of the 1931 *The Sittaford Mystery*); the short story has only recently been published in the UK for fear of giving away the ending. The play was originally called *Three Blind Mice*, but was soon changed to *The Mousetrap* (after *Hamlet*'s 'play within a play') to avoid clashing with a similarly titled production. Theatrical entrepreneur Peter Saunders oversaw its initial run at the Ambassadors Theatre, London, before moving it to the slightly larger St Martins Theatre, next door, on 25 March 1974. After eight years, a system was introduced of changing the cast and director annually, and by 1958 it had broken box-office records for being the longest running play in London – It celebrated its 25,000th performance on 18 November 2012, weeks after its Diamond Jubilee. An officially endorsed version of the play now tours the UK, alongside the uninterrupted London production. All the profits from it go to Christie's grandson Mathew Prichard.
Verdict: It has been said that *The Mousetrap* is not great, merely good enough, and that's a pretty fair description of this record-breaking theatrical anomaly. World War III aside, it will probably run forever, despite any amount of critical drubbing. 3/5

8. Witness for the Prosecution (1953)

Cast: Rosalie Westwater, Walter Horsbrugh, Milton Rosmer, Derek Blomfield, David Horne, David Raven, Percy Marmont, Patricia Jessel, Rosemary Wallace
Crew: Director Wallace Douglas
Premiere: 28 October 1953 (UK), 16 December 1954 (US).
Observations: This is a dramatisation of a short story from the 1933 collection *The Hound of Death*, but with a significantly altered dénouement. Christie considered it her most successful work.
Verdict: A brilliant piece of stagecraft. **5/5**

9. Spider's Web (1954)

Cast: Margaret Lockwood, John Warwick, Felix Aylmer, Harold Scott, Myles Eason
Crew: Director Wallace Douglas
Premiere: 13 December 1954.
Observations: Tailor-made for actress Margaret Lockwood, this production marked the first stage performance of an original Christie theatre script, at the time her third simultaneous London play.
Verdict: An unassuming comedy-thriller. **4/5**

10. A Daughter's a Daughter (1956)

Cast: Trevor Bannister, Margaret Gibson, Kathleen Cravos, Peter Henchie, Mary Manson, Audrey Noble, Henry Rayner, Daphne Riggs
Crew: Director Maurice Jones
Premiere: 9 July 1956.
Observations: This started out as an unperformed play written in the 1930s, before Christie reworked it into a 1952 novel, under the pseudonym Mary Westmacott. This updated stage version, produced by Peter Saunders, only ran for eight performances at the Theatre Royal, Bath.
Verdict: This strong drama would undoubtedly have made for a diverting evening's entertainment, but alas it was never going to be as popular as one of the author's whodunits. **3/5**

11. Towards Zero (1956)

Cast: Cyril Raymond, Mary Law, Gillian Lind, Frederick Leister, George Baker, Janet Barrow, Gwen Cherrell, Michael Scott, William Kendall

Crew: Director Murray MacDonald, Script Agatha Christie & Gerald Verner
Premiere: 4 September 1956.
Observation: For the only time in her career Christie collaborated with another writer for this adaptation of her 1944 novel.
Verdict: A reasonable effort, but the dialogue is occasionally stilted. **3/5**

12. Verdict (1958)

Cast: George Roubicek, Gretchen Franklin, Patricia Jessel, Gerald Heinz, Derek Oldham, Viola Keats, Moira Redmond, Norman Claridge, Michael Golden, Gerald Sim
Crew: Director Charles Hickman
Premiere: 22 May 1958.
Observations: Unusually this is not a whodunit, and so was not as successful as some of Christie's other plays. An error on the first night had the curtain falling too soon, thus completely changing the ending.
Verdict: Worthy, but uninspiring. **2/5**

13. The Unexpected Guest (1958)

Cast: Philip Newman, Renee Asherson, Nigel Stock, Winifred Oughton, Christopher Sandford, Violet Farebrother, Paul Curran, Michael Golden, Tenniel Evans
Crew: Director Hubert Gregg
Premiere: 12 August 1958.
Observations: Written quickly as a replacement for the ailing *Verdict*, this original stage play was received far more enthusiastically than its predecessor. A novelization by Charles Osborne appeared in 1999.
Verdict: Taught, insightful and full of surprises; the author is once more back on form. **5/5**

14. Go Back for Murder (1960)

Cast: Robert Urquhart, Peter Hutton, Ann Firbank, Mark Eden, Anthony Marlow, Laurence Hardy
Crew: Director Hubert Gregg
Premiere: 23 March 1960.
Observation: Based on *Five Little Pigs* (1943), Christie once again excluded Poirot from the cast.
Verdict: A curiously unexciting effort. **2/5**

15. Rule of Three (1962)

Cast: Betty McDowall, Mercy Haystead, David Langton, Raymond Bowers, Michael Beint, Robert Raglan, Mabelle George, Vera Cook, John Quayle, John Abineri, Margot Boyd
Crew: Director Hubert Gregg
Premiere: 20 December 1962.
Observations: 'The Rats', 'Afternoon at the Seaside' and 'The Patient' were the titles of the three one-act plays in this triple bill, the only time Christie would write in this form.
Verdict: Christie's stories always work better as full-length works, and the three playlets here are not among her best. **2/5**

16. Fiddlers Three (1972)

Cast: Doris Hare, Raymond Francis, Arthur Howard
Crew: Director Allan Davis
Premiere: 1 August 1972.
Observations: Christie's final play, *Fiddlers Five*, toured the provinces in 1971; this was then altered slightly (two main characters being merged into one) for its appearance as *Fiddlers Three* at the Yvonne Arnaud Theatre in Guildford. It never reached the West End.
Verdict: A slight, inconsequential piece – a sad end to a distinguished theatrical career. **2/5**

17. Chimneys (2003)

Cast & Crew: unknown
Premiere: 16 October 2003 (Canada), 1 June 2006 (UK).
Observations: Christie wrote this play, an adaptation of her 1925 spy thriller *The Secret of Chimneys*, in 1931 but for reasons unknown it was never performed. Considered 'lost' until 2001, a manuscript was discovered in the British Library and it received its world premiere at the Vertigo Theatre in Calgary as part of their Mystery Theatre series.
Verdict: Not a particularly enthralling adaptation of a fairly routine light-hearted thriller; mainly of interest for its relatively recent discovery. **2/5**

17

Radio and Television Plays

5 plays

1. Wasp's Nest (1937)

Cast: Francis L Sullivan
Crew: Producer George More O'Ferrall
TV Broadcast: 1937, BBC's Theatre Parade (25m)
Observations: This is the only television adaptation Christie wrote, an adaptation of her 1929 short story that later appeared in *Double Sin* (1961*).
Verdict: Primitive stuff, but fascinating to see Christie writing for a medium she would quickly grow to despise. **3/5**

2. Yellow Iris (1937)

Cast & Crew: unknown
Radio Broadcast: 2 November 1937, The Light Programme (duration unknown)
Observations: This is an adaptation of the short story that appeared in *The Regatta Mystery* (1939*). It was first performed on stage in the 2009 touring production *Murder on Air* produced by the Agatha Christie Theatre Company.
Verdict: By all accounts a fairly good dramatisation. **4/5**

3. Three Blind Mice (1947)

Cast: Barry Morse, Gladys Young, Raf de la Torre
Crew: Producer Martyn C Webster
Radio Broadcast: 26 May 1947, The Light Programme (30m)
Observations: Written to commemorate the 80th birthday of Queen Mary, Christie turned this radio play into a short story, published in 1950, before using it as the basis for the long-running stage play *The Mousetrap* (1952 onwards).

Verdict: Radio is probably the best medium for this claustrophobic tale. **5/5**

4. Butter in a Lordly Dish (1948)

Cast: Richard Williams, Lydia Sherwood, Cecile Chevreau
Crew: Producer Martyn C Webster
Radio Broadcast: 13 January 1948, The Light Programme (90m)
Observations: This rather grisly play was performed on stage in the 2009 touring production *Murder on Air* produced by the Agatha Christie Theatre Company.
Verdict: Well-written dialogue coupled with a clever plot. **5/5**

5. Personal Call (1954)

Cast: Jessie Evans, James McKenchnie, Mary Wimbush, Joan Sanderson, Hamilton Dyce
Crew: Producer Ayton Whitaker
Radio Broadcast: 31 May 1954, The Light Programme (30m)
Observations: The last radio play that Christie wrote, this concerns the mysterious death of a woman under the wheels of a train. It was first performed on stage in the 2009 touring production *Murder on Air* produced by the Agatha Christie Theatre Company.
Verdict: Not the greatest story, but it works well enough. **3/5**

18

Adaptations by Others – Theatre

The following is a list of all the major Agatha Christie theatre adaptations not written by the author herself. Only original casts are given. The premiere refers to the first known performance of the play – if unknown then the first major (normally West End) opening. American details are not given, whilst provincial and amateur productions are also excluded.

1. Alibi (1928)

Cast: Charles Laughton (Poirot), Lady Tree, Jane Welsh, Norman V Norman, Henry Daniell, Basil Loder, Iris Noel, Henry Forbes-Robertson, Gillian Lind, JH Roberts, Cyril Nash, John Darwin
Crew: Director Charles Laughton, Script Michael Morton
Premieres: 15 May 1928 (UK), 9 February 1932 (US).
Observations: This, the first Christie stage play, was an adaptation of *The Murder of Roger Ackroyd* (1926) minus the key character of Caroline Sheppard. In America the play was known as *The Fatal Alibi*.
Verdict: Laughton appears to have been popular, but the abstract nature of the plotting left many people unmoved. **3/5**

2. Love from a Stranger (1936)

Cast: Muriel Aked, Norait Howard, Marie Ney, Frank Vosper, Geoffrey King, Charles Hodges, Esma Cannon
Crew: Director Murray MacDonald, Script Frank Vosper
Premieres: 31 March 1936 (UK), 21 September 1936 (US).
Observations: A successful adaptation of 'Philomel Cottage' (from *The Listerdale Mystery*, 1934†), this stage thriller only ran for 31 performances in America (as opposed to almost 150 in England).
Verdict: A well-crafted horror story characterised by a masterful last act. **5/5**

3. Peril at End House (1940)

Cast: Francis L Sullivan (Poirot), Ian Fleming, Wilfred Fletcher, Donald Bisset, Tully Comber, Phoebe Kershaw, Olga Edwards, William Senior, Beckett Bould, Josephine Middleton, Isabel Dean
Crew: Director AR Whitmore, Script Arnold Ridley
Premiere: 2 January 1940.
Observations: Later staged at the Vaudeville Theatre, London, this was a straightforward adaptation of Christie's 1932 novel by Arnold Ridley, writer of the evergreen play *The Ghost Train* and famous as the bumbling Private Godfrey in the television series *Dad's Army* (1968–77). Sullivan returned to the rôle he had first played a decade earlier.
Verdict: A watertight version of one of the less interesting Poirot novels. **4/5**

4. Murder at the Vicarage (1949)

Cast: Barbara Mullen, Jack Lambert, Genine Graham, Michael Newell, Betty Sinclair, Michael Darbyshire, Andea Lea, Mildred Cottell, Alvys Mabon, Reginald Tate
Crew: Director Reginald Tate, Script Moie Charles & Barbara Toy
Premiere: 14 December 1949.
Observations: This is the first Miss Marple stage adaptation, based on her first print appearance in 1930. The setting was updated to the 1940s.
Verdict: A faithful version of the book with all its red herrings and counter-confessions. **3/5**

5. A Murder is Announced (1977)

Cast: Dulcie Gray (Miss Marple), Patricia Brake, Dinah Sheridan, Eleanor Summerfield, Christopher Scoular, Mia Nadasi, Barbara Flynn, Nancy Nevinson, Michael Dyerball, James Grout
Crew: Director Robert Chetwyn, Script Leslie Darbon
Premiere: 21 September 1977.
Observations: An adaptation of the 1950 novel.
Verdict: A faithful re-enactment of a popular book. **4/5**

6. Cards on the Table (1981)

Cast: Lynnett Edwards, William Eedle, Margaret Courtenay, Belinda Carroll, Pauline Jameson, Derek Waring, Gary Raymond, Gordon

Jackson, Charles Wallace, James Harvey, Mary Tamm
Crew: Director Peter Dews, Script Leslie Darbon
Premiere: 9 December 1981.
Observations: Although based on the 1936 novel, Poirot and Colonel Race are both excised from the narrative.
Verdict: A rather dull production of a notoriously static story. **3/5**

7. Murder is Easy (1993)

Cast: Nigel Davenport, Peter Capaldi, Charlotte Attenborough
Crew: Director Wyn Jones, Script Clive Exton
Premiere: 23 February 1993.
Observations: This was an adaptation of Christie's 1939 novel by *Poirot* scriptwriter Clive Exton. It ran for six weeks at the Duke of York's Theatre in London.
Verdict: A faithful adaptation of one Christie's lesser known plays, although critics were less than enthused. **4/5**

8. The Secret Adversary (2015)

Cast: Gamon Rhys (Tommy), Emerald O'Hanrahan (Tuppence), Keiran Buckeridge, Nigel Lister, Elizabeth Marsh, Morgan Philpott, Sophie Scott
Crew: Director Sarah Punshon, Script Sarah Punshon & Johann Hari
Premiere: 12 February 2015.
Observations: This new version of Christie's 1922 novel starring Tommy and Tuppence Beresford opened at the Watermill Theatre in Newbery, Berkshire, before touring the UK.
Verdict: An enjoyable stage version of this very early Christie. Despite suffering a slight identity crises – is it gentle pastiche or arch spoof? – the evening flies by. **4/5**

19

Adaptations by Others – Film

The following is a list of all the major Agatha Christie films released theatrically. The author herself never wrote a film screenplay. Foreign language productions are not included. Unless otherwise stated, the films are in colour.

Margaret Rutherford as Miss Marple

Born in Balham, London, on 11 May 1892, Margaret Rutherford pursued a highly successful acting career playing frumpy eccentric dowagers or dotty spinster aunts, usually with a humorous edge. She studied at the Old Vic School and began her stage career at the age of 33. Her most memorable screen rôle, apart from Miss Marple, was as Madame Arcati in David Lean's *Blithe Spirit* (1945), a part she played in the original Noël Coward stage production. She was awarded the OBE in 1961 and won an Oscar for her supporting role in *The VIPs* in 1963. In 1967 she was made a Dame Commander (DBE). She died on 22 May 1972 at Chalfont St Peter, Bucks, aged 80.

1. Murder She Said (1961)

Cast: Arthur Kennedy, Muriel Pavlow, James Robertson Justice, Charles Tingwell, Ronald Howard, Thorley Walters, Conrad Philips, Ronnie Raymond, Stringer Davis, Joan Hickson, Michael Golden, Richard Briers
Crew: Director George Pollack, Screenplay David D Osborn, David Pursall & Jack Seddon, Producer George H Brown (MGM, b/w, 86m)
Observations: Although admired by Christie as an actress, the author felt Rutherford was miscast as the elderly sleuth in this dramatisation of her 1957 novel *4.50 from Paddington*. The character of Elspeth McGillicuddy was eliminated from the screenplay to allow Rutherford greater screen presence. Her husband Stringer Davis joined her in all

four films. Joan Hickson, a later Miss Marple, was also in the cast.
Verdict: Lightweight fun. **4/5**

2. Murder at the Gallop (1963)

Cast: Robert Morley, Dame Flora Robson, Charles Tingwell, Stringer Davis, Duncan Lamont, Katya Douglas, James Villiers, Robert Urquhart, Gordon Harris, Kevin Stoney
Crew: Director George Pollock, Screenplay David Pursall, Jack Seddon & James P Cavanagh, Producers Lawrence P Bachmann & George H Brown (MGM, b/w, 81m)
Observations: The filmmakers chose to adapt a Hercule Poirot story, *After the Funeral* (1953), replacing the Belgian detective with his arch-rival Miss Marple! Apparently Christie was not amused.
Verdict: Despite the bastardised storyline, this is probably the best of the Rutherford Marples. **5/5**

3. Murder Most Foul (1964)

Cast: Ron Moody, Charles Tingwell, Megs Jenkins, James Bolam, Stringer Davis, Francesca Annis, Andrew Cruickshank, Ralph Michael, Allison Seebohm, Dennis Price, Terry Scott
Crew: Director George Pollock, Screenplay David Pursall & Jack Seddon, Producers Lawrence P Bachmann & Ben Arbeid (MGM, b/w, 90m)
Observations: In the manner of the previous film, another Poirot novel – *Mrs McGinty's Dead* (1952) – is turned into a Miss Marple vehicle, with the new name mirroring Christie's own idea of a "rotten" title (read 'Mr Eastwood's Adventure' from *The Listerdale Mystery*, 1934†). It received a delayed release in America, arriving the year after the fourth film, *Murder Ahoy!* (1964).
Verdict: Not as fresh as the first two, but still with some amusing moments. **3/5**

4. Murder Ahoy! (1964)

Cast: Charles Tingwell, Lionel Jeffries, Stringer Davis, William Mervyn, Francis Matthews, Nicholas Parsons, Derek Nimmo, Terence Edmond, Joan Benham, Gerald Cross
Crew: Director George Pollock, Screenplay David Pursall & Jack Seddon, Producer Lawrence P Bachmann (MGM, b/w, 74m)
Observations: The last in the MGM Rutherford series, this has

the distinction of being the only Agatha Christie film or television programme that is not based on a novel, short story or play.

Verdict: One has only to look at the cast to see this is being written and performed solely for laughs (which as a rule don't occur). The weakest of the series. **2/5**

Austin Trevor as Hercule Poirot

Born Austin Schilsky on 7 October 1897 in Belfast, Northern Ireland, Trevor was a popular British actor with a distinguished stage and film career. His forte was playing continental characters. Amongst his many film appearances, he could be seen in *Goodbye Mr Chips* (1939), *The Red Shoes* (1948), *The Day the Earth Caught Fire* (1961), *Konga* (1961) and the BBC series *Quatermass II* in 1955. He died in London on 22 January 1978.

1. Alibi (1931)

Cast: JH Roberts, Mercia Swinburne, Franklin Dyall, Elizabeth Allan, John Deverell, Ronald Ward, Mary Jerrold
Crew: Director Leslie Hiscott, Screenplay H Fowler Mear, Producer Julius Hagen (Twickenham Film Studios, b/w, 75m)
Observations: This film was based on the 1928 stage play of the same name, itself a dramatisation of *The Murder of Roger Ackroyd* (1926).
Verdict: Sans moustache, Austin Trevor looks nothing like Christie's Poirot! **3/5**

2. Black Coffee (1931)

Cast: Richard Cooper, Melville Cooper, Adrienne Allen, Elizabeth Allan, CV France, Philip Strange, Dino Galvani, Michael Shepley
Crew: Director Leslie Hiscott, Screenplay Brock Williams & H Fowler Mear, Producer Julius Hagen (Twickenham Film Studios, b/w, 78m)
Observations: The first Poirot film to feature Hastings and Japp, this was a filmed version of Christie's 1930 play of the same name.
Verdict: A well-received second outing for Trevor. **4/5**

3. Lord Edgware Dies (1934)

Cast: Richard Cooper, CV France, Jane Carr, John Turnbull, Michael Shepley, Leslie Perrins, Esme Percy
Director: Leslie Edwards, Screenplay H Fowler Mear, Producer Julius Hagen (Real Art Studios, b/w, 81m)
Observations: The last of the three Austin Trevor films, this is a straightforward adaptation of Christie's 1933 book. Poirot would not return to cinemas until 1966's *The Alphabet Murders*.
Verdict: In terms of professionalism, the best of the three films. **5/5**

Peter Ustinov as Hercule Poirot

Born in London on 16 April 1921 of French-speaking Russian parents, Ustinov was best known as a witty character actor and dazzling raconteur. He began acting at 17 and directed his first film at 25 (*School for Secrets*, 1946). He was Oscar nominated for his rôle as Nero in *Quo Vadis* (1951), and later won Academy Awards for his supporting rôles in *Spartacus* (1960) and *Topkapi* (1964); he has also won three Emmies for his outstanding contribution to television. He was made CBE in 1975 and knighted in 1990; since 1971 he was a tireless ambassador for UNICEF. He died on 28 March 2004.

1. Death on the Nile (1978)

Cast: David Niven, Mia Farrow, Lois Chiles, Simon MacCorkindale, Bette Davis, Maggie Smith, Olivia Hussey, Jane Birkin, Angela Lansbury, Jack Warden, George Kennedy
Crew: Director John Guillermin, Screenplay Anthony Shaffer, Producers John Brabourne & Richard Goodwin (EMI, 140m)
Observations: Filmed on location in Egypt, this adaptation of the 1937 novel is a sumptuous follow-up to the producers' box-office hit *Murder on the Orient Express* (1974). Because Albert Finney priced himself out of the film's budget, Peter Ustinov was cast as Poirot. Angela Lansbury later appeared as Miss Marple in the 1980 film *The Mirror Crack'd*.
Verdict: Despite Ustinov being far too portly to play the diminutive detective, the all-star cast and glossy settings virtually guarantee foolproof entertainment. **5/5**

2. Evil Under the Sun (1982)

Cast: Diana Rigg, Roddy McDowall, Maggie Smith, Jane Birkin, Colin Blakely, Nicholas Clay, Sylvia Miles, James Mason, Dennis Quilley
Crew: Director Guy Hamilton, Screenplay Anthony Shaffer, Producers John Brabourne & Richard Goodwin (EMI, 116m)
Observations: A follow-up to *Death on the Nile*, the filmmakers took their all-star cast to the island of Majorca (representing an island in the Adriatic) for this dramatisation of Christie's 1941 novel.
Verdict: A jarring mix of sun-drenched location footage and drab studio sets, any dramatic tension is ruined by inappropriately jolly music and Ustinov's questionable comic performance. **2/5**

3. Appointment with Death (1988)

Cast: Sir John Gielgud, Piper Laurie, Nicholas Guest, Carrie Fisher, John Terlesky, Valerie Richards, Amber Bezer, David Soul, Jenny Seagrove, Lauren Bacall, Hayley Mills
Crew: Director & Producer Michael Winner, Screenplay Anthony Shaffer, Michael Winner & Peter Buckman (Cannon, 108m)
Observations: Based loosely on Christie's 1938 novel, many familiar faces return for this final big-screen outing for Peter Ustinov.
Verdict: It's made by Michael Winner – need I say more? **1/5**

Miscellaneous

1. Die Abenteuer GmbH (1928)

Cast: Carlo Aldini, Eve Gray, Mikhail Rasumny, Hans Mierendorff, Hilda Bayley, Jack Mylong-Münz
Crew: Director Fred Sauer, Screenplay Jane Bess (Orplid-Film, b/w, silent, c90m)
Observations: Loosely translated as *Adventures Inc* or *Adventure Inc* (but not *Adventurers Inc* as some sources claim), this is the first Christie film adaptation, a silent German version of *The Secret Adversary* (1922).
Verdict: Overlong perhaps, but apparently an excellent stab at a full-length dramatisation. **4/5**

2. The Passing of Mr Quinn (1928)

Cast: Vivian Baron, Stewart Rome, Trilby Clark, Clifford Heatherley, Ursula Jeans
Crew: Director & Producer Julius Hagen, Screenplay Leslie Hiscott (Strand Films, b/w, silent, 100m)
Observations: This is a very loose adaptation of 'The Coming of Mr Quin' from *The Mysterious Mr Quin* (1930), as typified by the title change and misspelling of 'Quin'.
Verdict: A resemblance to Christie's story is presumably accidental. 2/5

3. Love from a Stranger (1937)

Cast: Basil Rathbone, Binnie Hale, Ann Harding, Bruce Seton, Jean Cadell, Bryan Powley, Joan Hickson
Crew: Director Rowland V Lee, Screenplay Frances Marion, Producer Max Schach (Trafalgar Studios, b/w, 87m)
Observations: Although filmed in England, this was to all intents and purposes a Hollywood production, with an American director who would go on to make *Son of Frankenstein* in 1939. It was based on Frank Vosper's stage play of the same name, itself adapted from the short story 'Philomel Cottage' (from *The Listerdale Mystery*, 1934†). Half a century later, Joan Hickson would play Miss Marple for the BBC TV series.
Verdict: A well-made thriller which still impresses today. 5/5

4. And Then There Were None (1945)

Cast: Walter Huston, Barry Fitzgerald, Louis Hayward, Roland Young, June Duprez, Sir C Aubrey Smith, Judith Anderson, Mischa Auer
Crew: Director & Producer René Clair, Screenplay Dudley Nichols (20th Century Fox, b/w, 97m)
Observations: Critically praised on its release, this was the first Christie film to be produced in Hollywood. Based on her own stage adaptation of the 1939 novel (with the resultant change of ending), it was released in the UK as *Ten Little Niggers*. Prince Starloff was not in the book or stage play.
Verdict: This is the first and undoubtedly the best of the many versions of this famous story. One of cinema's greatest murder mysteries, it's a production that exudes quality from every frame. 5/5

5. Love from a Stranger (1947)

Cast: John Hodiak, Sylvia Sidney, Ann Richards, John Howard, Isobel Elsom, Ernest Cossart, Anita Sharp-Bolster, Frederick Worlock
Crew: Director Richard Whorf, Screenplay Philip MacDonald, Producer James J Geller (Eagle Lion Films, b/w, 80m)
Observations: Known in the UK as *A Stranger Walked In*, this is a remake of 'Philomel Cottage', a short story from *The Listerdale Mystery* (1934†) collection. Mystery writer Philip MacDonald wrote the screenplay, which saw the ending and almost every character's name arbitrarily changed.
Verdict: Inferior in almost every way to the original film version. **2/5**

6. Witness for the Prosecution (1957)

Cast: Tyrone Power, Marlene Dietrich, Charles Laughton, Elsa Lanchester, John Williams, Henry Daniell, Ian Wolfe, Una O'Connor
Crew: Director Billy Wilder, Screenplay Billy Wilder, Harry Kurnitz & Larry Marcus, Producer Arthur Hornblow Jnr (United Artists, b/w, 114m)
Observations: Nominated for six Oscars, this was a hugely popular and successful adaptation of the hit 1953 stage play (based on a short story in *The Hound of Death*, 1933†). Christie sold the rights to United Artists for £116,000, and in the first year alone the film achieved US box-office takings of $3.7m.
Verdict: Inventive, witty, hypnotically engaging, this is a superb production with many of the all-star cast giving once-in-a-lifetime performances. **5/5**

7. The Spider's Web (1960)

Cast: Glynis Johns, John Justin, Jack Hulbert, Dame Cicely Courtneidge, Ronald Howard, David Nixon, Wendy Turner, Joan Sterndale-Bennett, Peter Butterworth
Crew: Director Godfrey Grayson, Screenplay Albert G Miller & Eldon Howard, Producers Edward J & Harry Lee Danziger (Danziger Studios, 89m)
Observations: This comedy-thriller was adapted from Christie's 1954 stage play *Spider's Web*. It was not released in the US.
Verdict: A comedy that only hits the mark if you're in an undiscerning mood. **2/5**

8. Ten Little Indians (1965)

Cast: Hugh O'Brian, Shirley Eaton, 'Fabian', Leo Genn, Stanley Holloway, Wilfrid Hyde-White, Daliah Lavi, Dennis Price, Mario Adorf, Marianne Hoppe

Crew: Director George Pollock, Screenplay Enrique Llovet, Dudley Nichols, Peter Welbeck (pseudonym of Harry Alan Towers), Peter Yeldham & Erich Kröhnke, Producer Harry Alan Towers (Seven Arts, b/w, 91m)

Observations: For this second film version of *Ten Little Niggers* (1939), the setting was changed from a remote island to a castle atop an Australian alp (but filmed in a disused mansion in Rush, near Dublin in Ireland). Various characters are new to this version, most noticeably teenage idol Fabian (real name: Fabiano Forte Bonaparte) as a rock and roll singer. To add novelty value, a 'whodunit break' was inserted towards the end to allow time for the audience to guess the identity of the killer.

Verdict: Entertaining enough in a kitsch sort of way, with the older cast members stealing every scene. **4/5**

9. The Alphabet Murders (1966)

Cast: Tony Randall (Poirot), Robert Morley, Anita Ekberg, Maurice Denham, Guy Rolfe, Sheila Allen, James Villiers, Julian Glover, Grazina Frame, Clive Morton, Cyril Luckham, Austin Trevor, Richard Wattis, Patrick Newell, Alison Seebohm, Windsor Davies, Sheila Reed, Dame Margaret Rutherford (Miss Marple), Stringer Davis

Crew: Director Frank Tashlin, Screenplay David Pursall & Jack Seddon, Producer Lawrence P Bachmann (MGM, 90m)

Observations: The classic 1936 novel *The ABC Murders* is used as the basis for this 'screwball comedy' by a director whose previous experience included Jerry Lewis and Bugs Bunny. Margaret Rutherford and Stringer Davis appeared in cameo rôles and Austin Trevor (cinema's first Poirot) appeared in his final film.

Verdict: Whoever thought they could turn Christie's fine thriller into this pathetic farce ought to be shot. Slowly. **1/5**

10. Endless Night (1971)

Cast: Hayley Mills, Hywel Bennett, Britt Ekland, Per Oscarsson, George Sanders, Peter Bowles, Lois Maxwell, Aubrey Richards, Ann Way, Patience Collier, Windsor Davies

Crew: Director & Screenplay Sidney Gilliat, Producer Leslie Gilliat (British Lion, 98m)

Observations: Location filming took place in France and Italy for this adaptation of Christie's 1967 book. One of George Sanders' final films before committing suicide, it was never released in America.

Verdict: Scary in parts, rather dull in others. **3/5**

11. Murder on the Orient Express (1974)

Cast: Albert Finney (Poirot), Lauren Bacall, Ingrid Bergman, Sean Connery, Sir John Gielgud, Martin Balsam, Jacqueline Bisset, Michael York, Jean Pierre Cassel, Dame Wendy Hiller, Anthony Perkins, Vanessa Redgrave, Rachel Roberts, Richard Widmark, Colin Blakely, George Coulouris, Denis Quilley

Crew: Director Sidney Lumet, Screenplay Paul Dehn, Producers John Brabourne & Richard Goodwin (EMI, 131m)

Observations: Filmed in genuine Orient Express cars borrowed from the Compagnie Internationale des Wagon-lits Museum in France, this lavish dramatisation of the 1934 novel was a massive critical and financial success. The film received six Oscar nominations, but only won one – Best Supporting Actress for Ingrid Bergman.

Verdict: Technically brilliant, this is probably the most successful Christie screen adaptation to date. **5/5**

12. And Then There Were None (1975)

Cast: Sir Richard Attenborough, Oliver Reed, Elke Sommer, Herbert Lom, Gert Frobe, Adolfo Celi, Charles Aznavour, Stephane Audran, Maria Rohm, Albert De Mendoza, Orson Welles

Crew: Director Peter Collinson, Screenplay Peter Welbeck (pseudonym of Harry Alan Towers), Producer Harry Alan Towers (Avco-Embassy Films, 98m)

Observations: For this third cinema version of *Ten Little Niggers* (1939) – known in the US as *Ten Little Indians* – the locale was again changed, this time to a luxurious hotel in the middle of the Iranian desert. The producer had worked in the same capacity on the 1965 film version, *Ten Little Indians*.

Verdict: An unwieldy international cast and listless direction handicap the screenplay, but there are some tense moments. **3/5**

13. Agatha (1979)

Cast: Vanessa Redgrave (Agatha Christie), Dustin Hoffman, Timothy Dalton, Helen Morse, Celia Gregory, Paul Brooke, Timothy West, Tony Britton
Crew: Director Michael Apted, Screenplay Kathleen Tynan & Arthur Hopcraft, Producers Jarvis Astaire & Gavrik Losey (Warner Bros, 98m)
Observations: This is an imaginative version of Agatha Christie's 1926 disappearance.
Verdict: A somewhat pointless dramatisation of a rather insignificant event, albeit good on period detail. **3/5**

14. The Mirror Crack'd (1980)

Cast: Angela Lansbury (Miss Marple), Elizabeth Taylor, Kim Novak, Geraldine Chaplin, Rock Hudson, Tony Curtis, Edward Fox, Marella Oppenheim, Wendy Morgan, Maureen Bennett, Pierce Brosnan, Charles Gray, Richard Pearson, Margaret Courtenay, Dinah Sheridan, Nigel Stock
Crew: Director Guy Hamilton, Screenplay Jonathan Hales & Barry Sandler, Producers John Brabourne & Richard Goodwin (EMI, 105m)
Observations: Despite its large roster of big names, this adaptation of the 1962 novel *The Mirror Crack'd from Side to Side* failed to do much business at the box office. Angela Lansbury had appeared in *Death on the Nile* (1978) and would go on to play a Miss Marple clone in the US television series *Murder She Wrote*.
Verdict: Waning Hollywood stars going through their motions as their careers fade behind them always makes for dispiriting viewing, and coupled with Lansbury's inappropriate youthfulness, the entire experience is one of ennui. **2/5**

15. Ordeal by Innocence (1985)

Cast: Donald Sutherland, Faye Dunaway, Ian McShane, Christopher Plummer, Sarah Miles, Anita Carey, Annette Crosbie, George Innes, Michael Maloney, Phoebe Nicholls, Diana Quick, Michael Elphick, Kevin Stoney, Brian Glover
Crew: Director Desmond Davis, Screenplay Alexander Stuart, Producer Jenny Craven (Cannon, 88m)
Observations: Shot in and around Dartmouth, Devon, this is a film version of one of Christie's favourite books, published in 1958.
Verdict: A run-of-the-mill adaptation with intrusive music. **2/5**

16. Ten Little Indians (1989)

Cast: Donald Pleasence, Herbert Lom, Brenda Vaccaro, Frank Stallone, Sarah Maur Thorp, Warren Berlinger, Yehuda Efroni, Neil McCarthy
Crew: Director Alan Birkinshaw, Screenplay Jackson Hunsicker & Gerry O'Hars, Producer Harry Alan Towers (Cannon, 100m)
Observations: For this fourth screen version of 1939's *Ten Little Niggers*, the setting is changed once again – to an African safari! Herbert Lom chalks up a second appearance in a remake of the 1945 original, and Donald Pleasence makes *his* second appearance of the year in a Christie story (the other being *A Caribbean Mystery* for the Joan Hickson BBC series). For the first time, the original 1930s period is correctly represented.
Verdict: Despite the odd setting, this is a surprisingly faithful rendition of the famous story. **4/5**

20

Adaptations by Others – Television

The following is a list of all major Agatha Christie television productions. Only first broadcast dates are noted; all are in the UK unless otherwise stated. Due to lack of space, some early black and white American productions have been excluded. For commercial channels, running times exclude advert breaks.

Peter Ustinov as Hercule Poirot

See 'Adaptations by Others – Films' for a biography.

1. Thirteen at Dinner (1985)

Cast: Jonathan Cecil, Allan Cuthbertson, Faye Dunaway, John Barron, Lee Horsley, Bill Nighy, Amanda Pays, Avril Elgar, Diane Keen, David Suchet, Benedict Taylor, David Frost
Crew: Director Lou Antonio, Teleplay Rod Browning, Producer Neil Hartley
US Broadcast: 18 October 1985, CBS (Warner Bros TV, 95m)
Observations: After two big-screen excursions, Peter Ustinov returns to the rôle of Poirot for this, the first of three TV adaptations. Notable in the cast is David Suchet as Inspector Japp who would go on to play the definitive Hercule Poirot for LWT. The title comes from the American name for *Lord Edgware Dies* (1933).
Verdict: A slick production with a strong cast. The best of the three Ustinovs. **5/5**

2. Dead Man's Folly (1986)

Cast: Jonathan Cecil, Jean Stapleton, Tim Pigott-Smith, Nicollette Sheridan, Constance Cummings, Susan Wooldridge, Ralph Arliss, Christopher Guard
Crew: Director Clive Donner, Teleplay Rod Browning, Producer Neil Hartley
US Broadcast: 8 January 1986, CBS (Warner Brothers Television, 95m)
Observations: This is a loose version of the 1956 novel.
Verdict: A passable adaptation, but it relies too heavily on comedy. **2/5**

3. Murder in Three Acts (1986)

Cast: Jonathan Cecil, Tony Curtis, Dana Elcar, Lee McCain, Diana Muldaur, Nicholas Pryor, Lisa Eichhorn, Emma Samms
Crew: Director Gary Nelson, Teleplay Scott Swanton, Producer Paul Waigner
US Broadcast: 30 September 1986, CBS (Warner Brothers Television, 95m)
Observations: Filmed in and around Acapulco, Mexico, this is an updated version of the original 1935 novel.
Verdict: Countless unnecessary changes made to characters and settings spoil what could have been an impressive production. **2/5**

David Suchet as Hercule Poirot

David Suchet was born in London on 2 May 1946. Since his first appearance in the BBC series *Oppenheimer* (1980), he has enjoyed a busy career playing character rôles of distinction in numerous films and television dramas.

Agatha Christie's Poirot (1989–2013)

The following *Poirot* episodes were produced by Clive Exton and Brian Eastman (1989–2002), and Michele Buck and Damien Timmer (2003–2013). The stories feature various recurring characters including Captain Hastings (Hugh Fraser), Chief Inspector Japp (Philip Jackson), Miss Lemon (Pauline Moran), Ariadne Oliver (Zoë Wanamaker) and Poirot's stolid valet George (David Yelland).

1. The Adventure of the Clapham Cook (1989)

Cast: Brigit Forsyth, Dermot Crowley, Freda Dowie, Antony Carrick, Katy Murphy, Daniel Webb
Crew: Director Edward Bennett, Teleplay Clive Exton
Broadcast: 8 January 1989, ITV (50m) – based on a short story from *The Under Dog* (1951*).

2. Murder in the Mews (1989)

Cast: Juliette Mole, David Yelland, James Faulkner, Gabrielle Blunt, John Cording, Barrie Cookson, Beccy Wright
Crew: Director Edward Bennett, Teleplay Clive Exton
Broadcast: 15 January 1989, ITV (50m) – based on the title story of the 1937 collection.

3. The Adventure of Johnnie Waverly (1989)

Cast: Geoffrey Bateman, Julia Chambers, Dominic Rougier, Patrick Jordan, Carol Frazer, Robert Putt
Crew: Director Renny Rye, Teleplay Clive Exton
Broadcast: 22 January 1989, ITV (50m) – based on a short story from *Three Blind Mice* (1950*).

4. Four and Twenty Blackbirds (1989)

Cast: Richard Howard, Tony Aitken, Charles Pemberton, Geoffrey Larder, Denys Hawthorn, Holly de Jong, Clifford Rose, Phillip Lacke, Hilary Mason, John Sessions
Crew: Director Renny Rye, Teleplay Russell Murray
Broadcast: 29 January 1989, ITV (50m) – based on a short story from *Three Blind Mice* (1950*).

5. The Third Floor Flat (1989)

Cast: Suzanne Burden, Nicholas Prichard, Robert Hines, Amanda Elwes, Josie Lawrence, Susan Porrett, James Aidan, Alan Partington
Crew: Director Edward Bennett, Teleplay Michael Baker
Broadcast: 5 February 1989, ITV (50m) – based on a short story from *Three Blind Mice* (1950*).

6. Triangle at Rhodes (1989)

Cast: Frances Low, Jon Cartwright, Annie Lambert, Peter Settelen, Angela Down, Timothy Knightley, Patrick Monckton, Al Fiorentini
Crew: Director Renny Rye, Teleplay Stephen Wakelam
Broadcast: 12 February 1989, ITV (50m) – based on a short story from *Murder in the Mews* (1937).

7. Problem at Sea (1989)

Cast: Sheila Allen, John Normington, Geoffrey Beevers, Melissa Greenwood, Ann Firbank, Roger Hume, Ben Aris, Caroline John
Crew: Director Renny Rye, Teleplay Clive Exton
Broadcast: 19 February 1989, ITV (50m) – based on a short story from *The Regatta Mystery* (1939*).

8. The Incredible Theft (1989)

Cast: John Stride, Carmen Du Sautoy, Ciaran Madden, John Carson, Phyllida Law
Crew: Director Edward Bennett, Teleplay David Reid & Clive Exton
Broadcast: 26 February 1989, ITV (50m) – based on a short story from *Murder in the Mews* (1937).

9. The King of Clubs (1989)

Cast: Niamh Cusack, David Swift, Gawn Grainger, Jonathan Coy, Jack Klaff, Avril Elgar, Sean Pertwee
Crew: Director Renny Rye, Teleplay Michael Baker
Broadcast: 5 March 1989, ITV (50m) – based on a short story in *The Under Dog* (1951*).

10. The Dream (1989)

Cast: Alan Howard, Joely Richardson, Mary Tamm, Martin Wenner, Christopher Saul, Paul Lacoux
Crew: Director Edward Bennett, Teleplay Clive Exton
Broadcast: 12 March 1989, ITV (50m) – based on a short story from *The Regatta Mystery* (1939*).

11. Peril at End House (1990)

Cast: Polly Walker, John Harding, Jeremy Young, Mary Cunningham, Paul Geoffrey, Alison Sterling, Christopher Baines, Carol MacReady, Elizabeth Downes
Crew: Director Renny Rye, Teleplay Clive Exton
Broadcast: 7 January 1990, ITV (100m) – based on the 1932 novel.

12. The Veiled Lady (1990)

Cast: Frances Barber, Terence Harvey, Carole Hayman
Crew: Director Edward Bennett, Teleplay Clive Exton
Broadcast: 14 January 1990, ITV (100m) – based on the short story from *Poirot Investigates* (1924).

13. The Lost Mine (1990)

Cast: Vincent Wong, Richard Albrecht, Anthony Bate, Colin Stinton, Barbara Barnes, James Saxon
Crew: Director Edward Bennett, Teleplay Michael Baker & David Renwick
Broadcast: 21 January 1990, ITV (50m) – based on a short story in *Poirot Investigates* (1924).

14. The Cornish Mystery (1990)

Cast: Amanda Walker, Tilly Vasburgh, Jerome Willis, Derek Benfield, John Bowler
Crew: Director Edward Bennett, Teleplay Clive Exton
Broadcast: 28 January 1990, ITV (50m) – based on a short story in *The Under Dog* (1951*).

15. The Disappearance of Mr Davenheim (1990)

Cast: Mel Martin, Kenneth Colley, Tony Mathews, Richard Beale
Crew: Director Andrew Grieve, Teleplay David Renwick
Broadcast: 4 February 1990, ITV (50m) – based on the short story found in *Poirot Investigates* (1924).

16. Double Sin (1990)

Cast: Adam Kotz, Paul Gabriel, Caroline Milmoe, David Hargreaves, Michael J Shannon, Amanda Garwood, Elspeth Gray
Crew: Director Richard Spence, Teleplay Clive Exton
Broadcast: 11 February 1990, ITV (50m) – based on the title story from the collection *Double Sin* (1961*).

17. The Adventure of the Cheap Flat (1990)

Cast: Samantha Bond, John Michie, Jenifer Landor, William Hootkins, Peter Howell, Nick Maloney, Ian Price
Crew: Director Richard Spence, Teleplay Russell Murray
Broadcast: 18 February 1990, ITV (50m) – based on a short story in *Poirot Investigates* (1924).

18. The Kidnapped Prime Minister (1990)

Cast: Timothy Block, Jack Elliot, David Horovitch, Lisa Harrow, Ronald Hines
Crew: Director Andrew Grieve, Teleplay Clive Exton
Broadcast: 25 February 1990, ITV (50m) – based on a short story from *Poirot Investigates* (1924).

19. The Adventure of the Western Star (1990)

Cast: Barry Woolgar, Bruce Montague, Struan Rodger, Rosalind Bennett, Oliver Cotton, Caroline Goodall, Alister Cameron
Crew: Director Richard Spence, Teleplay Clive Exton
Broadcast: 4 March 1990, ITV (50m) – based on a short story in *Poirot Investigates* (1924).

20. The Mysterious Affair at Styles (1990)

Cast: David Rintoul, Anthony Calf, Beatie Edney, Gillian Barge, Michael Cronin, Joanna McCallum, Allie Byrne, Morris Perry, Tim Munro, Tim Preece
Crew: Director Ross Devenish, Teleplay Clive Exton
Broadcast: 16 September 1990, ITV (100m) – based on the 1920 novel.

21. How Does Your Garden Grow? (1991)

Cast: Catherine Russell, Anne Stallybrass, Tim Wylton, Margery Masson, Ralph Nossek, Peter Birch, Dorcas Morgan
Crew: Director Brian Farnham, Teleplay Andrew Marshall
Broadcast: 6 January 1991, ITV (50m) – based on the short story from *The Regatta Mystery* (1939*).

22. The Million-Dollar Bond Robbery (1991)

Cast: Oliver Parker, Natalie Ogle, Ewan Hooper, David Quilter, Paul Young, Lizzy McInnerny, Kieron Jecchinis
Crew: Director Andrew Grieve, Teleplay Anthony Horowitz
Broadcast: 13 January 1991, ITV (50m) – based on the short story from *Poirot Investigates* (1924).

23. The Plymouth Express (1991)

Cast: John Stone, Marion Bailey, Alfredo Michelson, Shelagh McLeod, Julian Wadham, Kenneth Haigh
Crew: Director Andrew Piddington, Teleplay Rod Beacham
Broadcast: 20 January 1991, ITV (50m) – based on a short story from *The Under Dog* (1951*)

24. Wasps' Nest (1991)

Cast: Martin Turner, Melanie Jessop, Peter Capaldi, Kate Lynn-Evans, John Boswall
Crew: Director Brian Farnham, Teleplay David Renwick
Broadcast: 27 January 1991, ITV (50m) – based on a short story from *Double Sin* (1961*).

25. The Tragedy at Marsdon Manor (1991)

Cast: Ralph Watson, Ian McCulloch, Geraldine Alexander, Anita Carey, Desmond Barrit, Neil Duncan, Edward Jewesbury
Crew: Director Renny Rye, Teleplay David Renwick
Broadcast: 3 February 1991, ITV (50m) – based on a short story from *Poirot Investigates* (1924).

26. The Double Clue (1991)

Cast: Kika Markham, David Lyon, Nicholas Selby, David Bamber, Charmian May, William Chubb, Michael Packer
Crew: Director Andrew Piddington, Teleplay Anthony Horowitz
Broadcast: 10 February 1991, ITV (50m) – based on a short story in *Double Sin* (1961*).

27. The Mystery of the Spanish Chest (1991)

Cast: John McEnery, Pip Torrens, Antonia Pemberton, Caroline Langrishe, Malcolm Sinclair, Peter Copley, Edward Clayton
Crew: Director Andrew Grieve, Teleplay Anthony Horowitz
Broadcast: 17 February 1991, ITV (50m) – based on a short story in *The Adventure of the Christmas Pudding* (1960†).

28. The Theft of the Royal Ruby (1991)

Cast: Nigel Le Vaillant, John Vernon, Frederick Treves, Stephanie Cole, David Howey, Tariq Alibai, Helena Michell, John Dunbar
Crew: Director Andrew Grieve, Teleplay Anthony Horowitz
Broadcast: 24 February 1991, ITV (50m) – based on the (American version of the) title story from *The Adventure of the Christmas Pudding* (1960†).

29. The Affair at the Victory Ball (1991)

Cast: Mark Crowdy, David Henry, Andrew Burt, Hadyn Gwynne, Nathaniel Parker, Natalie Slater, Kate Harper
Crew: Director Renny Rye, Teleplay Andrew Marshall
Broadcast: 3 March 1991, ITV (50m) – based on a short story from *The Under Dog* (1951*)

30. The Mystery of Hunter's Lodge (1991)

Cast: Roy Boyd, Bernard Horsfall, Jim Norton, Diana Kent, Shaughan Seymour, Victoria Alcock, Clare Travers-Deacon, Christopher Scoular
Crew: Director Renny Rye, Teleplay TR Bowen
Broadcast: 10 March 1991, ITV (50m) – based on a short story in *Poirot Investigates* (1924).

31. The ABC Murders (1992)

Cast: David McAlister, Allan Mitchell, Cathryn Bradshaw, Michael Mellinger, John Breslin, Nicholas Farrell, Nina Marc, Donald Douglas, Donald Sumpter, Pippa Guard, Vivienne Forbes, Ann Windsor
Crew: Director Andrew Grieve, Teleplay Clive Exton
Broadcast: 5 January 1992, ITV (100m) – based on the classic 1936 novel.

32. Death in the Clouds (1992)

Cast: Sarah Woodward, Shaun Scott, Richard Ireson, David Firth, Cathryn Harrison, Amanda Royle, Eve Pearce, Jenny Downham, Roger Heathcott, Guy Manning, Gabrielle Lloyd, John Bleasdall
Crew: Director Stephen Whittaker, Teleplay William Humble
Broadcast: 12 January 1992, ITV (100m) – based on the 1935 novel.

33. One, Two, Buckle My Shoe (1992)

Cast: Carolyn Colquhoun, Joanna Phillips-Lane, Peter Blythe, Joe Greco, Christopher Eccleston, Karen Gledhill, Laurence Harrington, Sara Stewart, Helen Horton, Kevork Malikyan, Trilby James
Crew: Director Ross Devenish, Teleplay Clive Exton
Broadcast: 19 January 1992 (100m) – based on the 1940 novel.

34. The Adventure of the Egyptian Tomb (1993)

Cast: Peter Reeves, Bill Bailey, Paul Birchard, Rolf Saxon, Oliver Pierre, Jon Strickland, Simon Cowell-Parker, Anna Cropper, Mozaffar Shafeir
Crew: Peter Barber-Fleming, Teleplay Clive Exton
Broadcast: 17 January 1993, ITV (50m) – based on a short story from *Poirot Investigates* (1924).

35. The Under Dog (1993)

Cast: Bill Wallis, Andrew Seear, Denis Lill, Ann Bell, Ian Gelder, Jonathan Phillips, Adie Allen
Crew: Director John Bruce, Teleplay Bill Craig
Broadcast: 24 January 1993, ITV (50m) – based on the title story from *The Under Dog* (1951*).

36. Yellow Iris (1993)

Cast: David Troughton, Geraldine Somerville, Hugh Ross, Stefan Gryff, Yolanda Vasquez, Robin McCaffrey, Joseph Long
Crew: Director Peter Barber-Fleming, Teleplay Anthony Horowitz
Broadcast: 31 January 1993, ITV (50m) – based on a short story from *The Regatta Mystery* (1939*) with the addition of Hastings and Miss Lemon.

37. The Case of the Missing Will (1993)

Cast: Mark Kingston, Terence Hardiman, Rowena Cooper, Edward Atterton, Gillian Hanna, Beth Goddard, Susan Tracy, Neil Stuke, Jon Laurimore
Crew: Director John Bruce, Teleplay Douglas Watkinson
Broadcast: 7 February 1993, ITV (50m) – based on a short story from *Poirot Investigates* (1924) with the addition of the Siddaways and Chief Inspector Japp.

38. The Adventure of the Italian Nobleman (1993)

Cast: David Neal, Anna Mazzotti, Sidney Kean, Vincenzo Ricotta, Leonard Preston, Janet Lees Price, Arthur Cox
Crew: Director Brian Farnham, Teleplay Clive Exton
Broadcast: 14 February 1993, ITV (50m) – based on the 1924 collection *Poirot Investigates*.

39. The Chocolate Box (1993)

Cast: Rosalie Crutchley, Anna Chancellor, James Coombes, Geoffrey Whitehead, David de Keyser, Jonathan Hackett, Mark Eden, Preston Lockwood
Crew: Director Ken Grieve, Teleplay Douglas Watkinson
Broadcast: 21 February 1993, ITV (50m) – loosely based on a short story in *Poirot Investigates* (1924) with Japp replacing Hastings.

40. Dead Man's Mirror (1993)

Cast: Zena Walker, Iain Cuthbertson, Richard Lintern, Fiona Walker, Emma Fielding, Tushka Bergen, Jeremy Northam
Crew: Director Brian Farnham, Teleplay Anthony Horowitz
Broadcast: 28 February 1993, ITV (50m) – based on a short story

from *Murder in the Mews* (1937) with Japp replacing Major Riddle and Satterthwaite (a character often associated with Harley Quin) disappearing entirely.

41. The Jewel Robbery at the Grand Metropolitan (1993)

Cast: Trevor Cooper, Sorcha Cusack, Hermione Norris, Karl Johnson, Elizabeth Rider, Simon Shepherd
Crew: Director Ken Grieve, Teleplay Anthony Horowitz
Broadcast: 7 March 1993, ITV (50m) – based on the short story from *Poirot Investigates* (1924).

42. Hercule Poirot's Christmas (1995)

Cast: Mark Tandy, Catherine Rabett, Simon Roberts, Brian Gwaspari, Sasha Behar, Eric Carte, Andree Bernard, Ayd Khan Din, Vernon Dobtcheff, Olga Lowe
Crew: Director Edward Bennett, Teleplay Clive Exton
Broadcast: 1 January 1995, ITV (100m) – based on the 1938 novel.

43. Hickory Dickory Dock (1995)

Cast: Paris Jefferson, Jonathan Firth, Damian Lewis, Granville Saxton, Gilbert Martin, Elinor Morriston, Polly Kemp, Sarah Badel, Rachel Bell, David Burke, Jessica Lloyd
Crew: Director Andrew Grieve, Teleplay Anthony Horowitz
Broadcast: 12 February 1995, ITV (100m) – based on the 1955 novel.

44. Murder on the Links (1996)

Cast: Bill Moody, Damien Thomas, Jacinta Mulcahy, Bernard Latham, Ben Pullen, Diana Fletcher, Terence Beesley, Kate Fahy
Crew: Director Andrew Grieve, Teleplay Anthony Horowitz
Broadcast: 11 February 1996, ITV (100m) – based on the second Poirot novel, published in 1923.

45. Dumb Witness (1997)

Cast: Patrick Ryecart, Kate Buffery, Norma West, Julia St John, Paul Herzberg, Ann Morish, Pauline Jameson, Muriel Pavlow
Crew: Director Edward Bennett, Teleplay Douglas Watkinson
Broadcast: 16 March 1997, ITV (100m) – based on the 1937 novel.

46. The Murder of Roger Ackroyd (2000)

Cast: Oliver Ford Davies, Selina Cadell, Malcolm Terris, Roger Frost, Nigel Cooke, Daisy Beaumont, Flora Montgomery, Vivien Heilbron
Crew: Director Andrew Grieve, Teleplay Clive Exton
Broadcast: 2 January 2000, ITV (100m) – based on the classic 1926 novel.

47. Lord Edgware Dies (2000)

Cast: John Castle, Helen Grace, Fiona Allen, Dominic Guard, Deborah Cornelius, Hannah Yelland, Tim Steed
Crew: Director Brian Farnham, Teleplay Anthony Horowitz
Broadcast: 19 February 2000, ITV (100m) – based on the 1933 novel.

48. Evil Under the Sun (2001)

Cast: Louise Delemere, Tim Meats, Tamzin Malleson, Michael Higgs, David Mallinson, Roger Alborough
Crew: Director Brian Farnham, Teleplay Anthony Horowitz
Broadcast: 20 April 2001, ITV1 (100m) – based on the 1941 novel.

49. Murder in Mesopotamia (2001)

Cast: Ron Berglas, Barbara Barnes, Dinah Stabb, Georgina Sowerby, Jeremy Turner-Welch, Pandora Clifford, Christopher Hunter, Christopher Bowen, Iain Mitchell, Alexi Kaye Campbell, Deborah Poplett
Crew: Director Tom Clegg, Teleplay Clive Exton
Broadcast: 8 July 2001, ITV1 (100m) – based on the 1936 novel.

50. Five Little Pigs (2003)

Cast: Toby Stephens, Sophie Winkleman, Gemma Jones, Julie Cox, Rachael Stirling, Aidan Gillen, Marc Warren, Patrick Malahide, Aimee Mullins, Annette Badland, Roger Brierley, Melissa Suffield, Talulah Riley
Crew: Director Paul Unwin, Teleplay Kevin Elyot
Broadcast: 14 December 2003, ITV1 (100m) – based on the 1943 novel.

51. Sad Cypress (2003)

Cast: Elisabeth Dermot-Walsh, Marion O'Dwyer, Rupert Penry-Jones, Paul McGann, Kelly Reilly, Phyllis Logan, Diana Quick, Stuart Laing, Linda Spurrier, Alistair Findlay, Louise Callaghan, Geoffrey Beevers, Ian Taylor, Jack Galloway, Timothy Carlton
Crew: Director Dave Moore, Teleplay David Pirie
Broadcast: 26 December 2003, ITV1 (100m) – based on the 1940 novel.

52. Death on the Nile (2004)

Cast: James Fox, Emma Malin, Emily Blunt, JJ Feild, Judy Parfitt, Daisy Donovan, Steve Pemberton, Alastair MacKenzie, Barbara Flynn, Daniel Lapaine, Frances de la Tour, Zoë Telford, David Soul, George Yiasoumi, Elodie Kendall, Felicite du Jeu
Crew: Director Andy Wilson, Teleplay Kevin Elyot
Broadcast: 12 April 2004, ITV1 (100m) – based on the 1937 novel.

53. The Hollow (2004)

Cast: Jonathan Cake, Megan Dodds, Edward Fox, Claire Price, Lysette Anthony, Lucy Briers, Harriet Cobbold, Edward Hardwicke, Teresa Churcher, Paula Jacobs, Tom Georgeson, Jamie de Courcey, Sarah Miles, Caroline Martin, Ian Talbot, Andrew Watson, Dale Rapley
Crew: Director Simon Langton, Teleplay Nick Dear
Broadcast: 26 April 2004, ITV1 (100m) – based on the 1946 novel.

54. The Mystery of the Blue Train (2006)

Cast: Elliott Gould, Tom Harper, Lindsay Duncan, Alice Eve, James D'Arcy, Jaime Murray, Nicholas Farrell, Bronagh Gallagher, Georgina Rylance, Oliver Milburn, Josette Simon, Roger Lloyd-Pack, Jane How, Samuel James, Helen Lindsay, Etela Pardo
Crew: Director Hettie Macdonald, Teleplay Guy Andrews
Broadcast: 1 January 2006, ITV1 (100m) – based on the 1928 novel.

55. Cards on the Table (2006)

Cast: Alexander Siddig, Alex Jennings, Tristan Gemmill, Lesley Manville, Lyndsey Marshal, Robert Pugh, David Westhead, Honeysuckle Weeks, Lucy Liemann, Philip Bowen, Cordelia Bugeja,

Zigi Ellison, Jennie Ogilvie, James Alper, Philip Wright, Douglas Reith
Crew: Director Sarah Harding, Teleplay Nick Dear
Broadcast: 19 March 2006, ITV1 (100m) – based on the 1936 novel.

56. After the Funeral (2006)

Cast: Robert Bathurst, Geraldine James, Michael Fassbender, Julian Ovenden, Monica Dolan, Fiona Glascott, Anthony Valentine, Lucy Punch, Benjamin Whitrow, Anna Calder-Marshall, Kevin Doyle, William Russell, Dominic Jephcott, John Carson, Annabel Scholey, Philip Anthony, Vicky Ogden
Crew: Director Maurice Phillips, Teleplay Philomena McDonagh
Broadcast: 26 March 2006, ITV1 (100m) – based on the 1953 novel.

57. Taken at the Flood (2006)

Cast: Jenny Agutter, Celia Imrie, Tim Pigott-Smith, Amanda Douge, Patrick Baladi, Eva Birthistle, Elliot Cowan, Penny Downie, Richard Durden, Claire Hackett, Richard Hope, Nicholas Le Prevost, Elizabeth Spriggs, Pip Torrens, Tim Woodward, David Yelland, Martha Barnett
Crew: Director Andy Wilson, Teleplay Guy Andrews
Broadcast: 2 April 2006, ITV1 (100m) – based on the 1948 novel.

58. Mrs McGinty's Dead (2008)

Cast: Simon Shepherd, Siân Philips, Joe Absolom, Simon Molloy, Richard Hope, David Yelland, Zoë Wanamaker, Sarah Smart, Raquel Cassidy, Richard Dillane, Emma Amos, Billy Geraghty, Ruth Gemmell, Mary Stockley, Paul Rhys, Catherine Russell, Amanda Root, Richard Lintern
Crew: Director Ashley Pearce, Teleplay Nick Dear
Broadcast: 14 September 2008, ITV1 (100m) – based on the 1952 novel.

59. Cat Among the Pigeons (2008)

Cast: Harriet Walter, Raji James, Adam De Ville, Anton Lesser, Don Gallagher, Georgie Glen, Georgia Cornick, Carol MacReady, Claire Skinner, Miranda Raison, Susan Wooldridge, Natasha Little, Amara Karan, Adam Croasdell, Amanda Abbington, Elizabeth Berrington, Jo Woodcock, Lois Edmett, Pippa Haywood, Jane How, Katie Leung
Crew: Director James Kent, Teleplay Mark Gatiss

Broadcast: 21 September 2008, ITV1 (100m) – based on the 1959 novel.

60. Third Girl (2008)

Cast: Peter Bowles, Haydn Gwynne, David Yelland, Zoë Wanamaker, Jemima Rooper, Clemency Burton-Hill, Matilda Sturridge, Tom Mison, Jarn Warnaby, Caroline O'Neill, James Wilby, Lucy Liemann, Tim Stern, Simon Hill, Tessa Bell-Briggs, Jade Longley, Juliet Howland
Crew: Director Dan Reed, Teleplay Peter Flannery
Broadcast: 28 September 2008, ITV1 (100m) – based on the 1966 novel.

61. Appointment with Death (2009)

Cast: Tim Curry, Cheryl Campbell, Jawad Elalami, Christina Cole, Tom Riley, Zoe Boyle, Emma Cunniffe, Angela Pleasence, Abdelkader Aizoun, Mark Gatiss, John Hannah, Paul Freeman, Beth Goddard, Christian McKay, Mansour Badri, Zakaria Atifi, Elizabeth McGovern
Crew: Director Ashley Pearce, Teleplay Guy Andrews
Broadcast: 25 December 2009, ITV1 (100m) – based on the 1938 novel.

62. Three Act Tragedy (2010)

Cast: Martin Shaw, Art Malik, Kimberley Nixon, Jane Asher, Anna Carteret, Suzanne Bertish, Anastasia Hille, Ronan Vibert, Kate Ashfield, Nigel Pegram, Tom Wisdom, Michael Hobbs, Jodie McNee, James Hurran, David Yelland, Tony Maudsley, Prue Clarke
Crew: Director Ashley Pearce, Teleplay Nick Dear
Broadcast: 3 January 2010, ITV1 (100m) – based on the 1935 novel.

63. Hallowe'en Party (2010)

Cast: Timothy West, Fenella Woolgar, Amelia Bullmore, Zoë Wanamaker, Deborah Findlay, Mary Higgins, Sophie Thompson, Georgia King, Ian Hallard, Phyllida Law, Eric Sykes, Julian Rhind-Tutt, Macy Nyman, Richard Breislin, David Yelland, Paola Dionisotti, Paul Thornley, Vera Filatova
Crew: Director Charles Palmer, Teleplay Mark Gatiss
Broadcast: 27 October 2010, ITV1 (100m) – based on the 1969 novel.

64. Murder on the Orient Express (2010)

Cast: David Morrissey, Toby Jones, Eileen Atkins, Barbara Hershey, Hugh Bonneville, Samuel West, Tristan Shepherd, Sam Crane, Brian J Smith, Jessica Chastain, Stewart Scudamore, Serge Hazanavicius, Susanne Lothar, Denis Ménochet, Marie-Josée Croze, Stanley Weber, Elena Satine, Joseph Mawle
Crew: Director Philip Martin, Teleplay Stewart Harcourt
Broadcast: 25 December 2010, ITV1 (100m) – based on the 1934 novel.

65. The Clocks (2011)

Cast: Lesley Sharp, Anna Massey, Phil Daniels, Geoffrey Palmer, Frances Barber, Guy Henry, Olivia Grant, Anna Skellern, Tom Burke, Andrew Havill, Victoria Wicks, Jaime Winstone, Sinead Keenan, Ben Righton, Beatie Edney, Abigail Thaw, Phoebe Strickland, Isabella Parriss, Tessa Peake-Jones, Jason Watkins, Stephen Boxer, Andrew Forbes
Crew: Director Charles Palmer, Teleplay Stewart Harcourt
Broadcast: 26 December 2011, ITV1 (100m) – based on the 1963 novel.

66. Elephants Can Remember (2013)

Cast: Greta Scacchi, Zoë Wanamaker, Adrian Lukis, Annabel Mullion, Iain Glen, Vincent Regan, Alexandra Dowling, Vanessa Kirby, Caroline Blakiston, Elsa Mollien, Maxine Evans, Jo-Anne Stockham, Hazel Douglas, Ferdinand Kingsley, Danny Webb, Claire Cox, Ruth Sheen
Crew: Director John Strickland, Teleplay Nick Dear
Broadcast: 9 June 2013, ITV (100m) – based on the 1972 novel, the last Poirot story that Christie wrote.

67. The Big Four (2013)

Cast: Hugh Fraser, Philip Jackson, David Yelland, Patricia Hodge, Sarah Parish, Pauline Moran, Tom Brooke, Nicholas Day, James Carroll Jordan, Steven Pacey, Simon Lowe, Michael Culkin, Lou Broadbent, Peter Symonds, Barbara Kirby, Nicholas Burns, Alex Palmer, Teresa Banham, Jack Farthing, Ian Hallard
Crew: Director Peter Lydon, Teleplay Mark Gatiss & Ian Hallard
Broadcast: 23 October 2013, ITV (100m) – based on the 1927 novel.

68. Dead Man's Folly (2013)

Cast: Sean Pertwee, Sinéad Cusack, Martin Jarvis, Rosalind Ayres, Rebecca Front, Zoë Wanamaker, Sam Kelly, Chris Gordon, Richard Dixon, Francesca Zoutewelle, Stephanie Leonidas, James Anderson, Emma Hamilton, Daniel Weyman, Ella Geraghty, Elliot Barnes-Worrell, Nicholas Woodeson, Tom Ellis, Angel Witney
Crew: Director Tom Vaughan, Teleplay Nick Dear
Broadcast: 30 October 2013, ITV (100m) – based on the 1956 novel.

69. The Labours of Hercules (2013)

Cast: Rupert Evans, Patrick Ryecart, Tom Chadbon, Simon Callow, Lorna Nickson Brown, Stephen Frost, Isobel Middleton, Tom Austen, Fiona O'Shaughnessy, Nicholas McGaughey, Tom Wlaschiha, Morven Christie, Sandy McDade, Orla Brady, Nigel Lindsay, Richard Katz, Eleanor Tomlinson
Crew: Director Andy Wilson, Teleplay Guy Andrews
Broadcast: 6 November 2013, ITV (100m) – based on the 1947 short story collection.

70. Curtain: Poirot's Last Case (2013)

Cast: Helen Baxendale, Hugh Fraser, Anne Reid, Philip Glenister, Shaun Dingwall, David Yelland, John Standing, Aidan McArdle, Adam Englander, Alice Orr-Ewing, Matthew McNulty, Anna Madeley, Claire Keelan, Gregory Cox
Crew: Director Hettie Macdonald, Teleplay Kevin Elyot
Broadcast: 13 November 2013, ITV (100m) – based on Poirot's 'final adventure', a novel written in the 1940s but not published until 1975.

Overall Verdict: The vast majority of these productions are skilful renderings of Christie's original stories, with the barest minimum of tinkering to put them on the screen. Only with *The Murder of Roger Ackroyd* does the quality slip, but then this was an impossible novel to dramatize whilst being faithful to the source material. As the stories progressed, the tone became darker, a reflection perhaps of television's obsession with the gloomier aspects of crime drama, influenced by such 'Nordic Noir' as *Wallender* (2005–present) and *The Killing* (2007–2012). However, the production team's dedication in adapting every single Poirot story, and Suchet's rock-solid performance in the central role, marks this as a benchmark for Christie on television. **5/5**.

Helen Hayes as Miss Marple

Born on 10 October 1900 in Washington DC, Helen Hayes made her sound film debut in *The Sin of Madelon Claudet* (1931). From then on she concentrated mainly on her theatrical career: she was nicknamed the 'First Lady of the American Theater'. Amongst her many awards was an Oscar for her rôle as the eccentric stowaway in *Airport* (1969). She died on 17 March 1993.

1. A Caribbean Mystery (1983)

Cast: Maurice Evans, Bernard Hughes, George Innes, Swoozie Kurtz, Jameson Parker, Season Hubley
Crew: Director Robert M Lewis, Teleplay Steve Humphrey & Sue Grafton, Producer Stan Marguiles
US Broadcast: 22 October 1983, CBS (Warner Bros TV, 97m)
Observations: Shot on location, this is a version of the 1964 novel featuring a cast of American television actors.
Verdict: A cheap TV movie that captures none of the atmosphere of the book. **2/5**

2. Murder With Mirrors (1985)

Cast: Bette Davis, John Mills, John Woodvine, Dorothy Tutin, James Coombs, Tim Roth, Christopher Fairbank, Leo McKern
Crew: Director Dick Lowry, Teleplay Richard Eckstein, Producer George Eckstein
US Broadcast: 20 February 1985, CBS (Warner Bros TV, 95m)
Observations: Based on the 1952 novel.
Verdict: Another dull adaptation. **2/5**

Joan Hickson as Miss Marple

Hickson was born on 5 August 1906 in Kingsthorpe, Northants and, like Margaret Rutherford, made a successful acting career of playing slightly dotty ladies (such as in *One of Our Dinosaurs is Missing*, 1976). It was while appearing in the 1946 play *Appointment with Death* that Agatha Christie sent her a note saying, "I hope one day you will play my dear Miss Marple." She was awarded an OBE in 1987 and died on 17 October 1998, aged 92.

Agatha Christie's Miss Marple (1984–1992)

1. The Body in the Library (1984)

Cast: Moray Watson, Gwen Watford, David Horovitch, Andrew Cruikshank, Keith Drinkel, Jess Conrad, Valentine Dyall, Frederick Jaeger
Crew: Director Silvio Narizzano, Teleplay TR Bowen, Producer Guy Slater
Broadcast: 26–28 December 1984, 3 parts, BBC1 (150m)
Observations: Joan Hickson was 79 when she took on the rôle she is probably most famous for. In this adroit adaptation of Christie's 1942 novel (the fourth Marple story), she became an instant success with critics and general public alike, prompting eleven further outings.

2. The Moving Finger (1985)

Cast: Andrew Bicknell, Michael Culver, Richard Pearson, John Arnatt, Dilys Hamlett, Gerald Sim, Martin Fisk, Sandra Payne, Victor Maddern
Crew: Director Roy Boulting, Teleplay Julia Jones, Producer Guy Slater
Broadcast: 21–22 February 1985, 2 parts, BBC1 (100m)
Observations: Based on Christie's fifth Marple book published in 1943, this is another excellent production. Despite Miss Marple's late entrance into the proceedings, the strong cast keeps the action moving nicely.

3. A Murder is Announced (1985)

Cast: Ursula Howells, Sylvia Sims, Ralph Michael, Joan Sims, David Collings, Renee Asherson, John Castle, Samantha Bond, Kevin Whately
Crew: Director David Giles, Teleplay Alan Plater, Producer Guy Slater
Broadcast: 28 February–2 March 1985, 3 parts, BBC1 (150m)
Observations: Based on the 1950 novel.

4. A Pocket Full of Rye (1985)

Cast: Timothy West, Martyn Stanbridge, Fabia Drake, Peter Davison, Clive Merrison, Stacy Dorning, Rachel Bell, Annette Badland
Crew: Director Guy Slater, Teleplay TR Bowen, Producer George Gallaccio
Broadcast: 7–8 March 1985, 2 parts, BBC1 (100m)

Observations: Timothy West had previously appeared as Kenward, the policeman in charge of finding Agatha Christie, in the 1979 feature film *Agatha*. Peter Davison went on to play the upper class sleuth Albert Campion in a cruelly short-lived BBC series based on the books of Margery Allingham.

5. Murder at the Vicarage (1986)

Cast: Paul Eddington, Cheryl Campbell, Robert Lang, Norma West, James Hazeldine, Tara MacGowan, Polly Adams, Christopher Good, Michael Browning, David Horovitch
Crew: Director Julian Amyes, Teleplay TR Bowen, Producer George Gallaccio
Broadcast: 25–26 December 1986, 2 parts, BBC1 (100m)
Observations: This dramatisation of Christie's first Miss Marple novel, which appeared in 1930, is another fine production. Paul Eddington is perfectly cast as the timorous vicar while the rest of the cast provide able support.

6. Sleeping Murder (1987)

Cast: Frederick Treves, Geraldine Alexander, John Moulder-Brown, Jean Anderson, Terrence Hardiman, Jack Watson, Jean Scott, John Bennett, Geraldine Newman, Kenneth Cope
Crew: Director John Howard Davies, Teleplay Ken Taylor, Producer George Gallaccio
Broadcast: 11–18 January 1987, 2 parts, BBC1 (100m)
Observations: Oddly, the BBC decided to dramatise the last published Miss Marple story halfway through its run. But unlike *Curtain: Poirot's Last Case* (1975), the 1976 *Sleeping Murder* has no death scene for the elderly detective, and it is quite conceivable that she went on to solve many further cases afterwards.

7. At Bertram's Hotel (1987)

Cast: Caroline Blakiston, James Cossins, Joan Greenwood, Helena Michell, George Baker, Philip Bretherton, Preston Lockwood, Irene Sutcliffe
Crew: Director Mary McMurray, Teleplay Jill Hyem, Producer George Gallaccio
Broadcast: 25 January 1987, BBC1 (120m)

Observations: George Baker was most famous for his rôle as Inspector Wexford in *The Wexford Mysteries*, and here is playing another of the kind in this impressive adaptation of the 1965 novel.

8. Nemesis (1987)

Cast: John Horsley, Peter Copley, Helen Cherry, Anna Cropper, Margaret Tyzack, Valerie Lush, Bruce Payne, Peter Tilbury
Crew: Director David Tucker, Teleplay TR Bowen, Producer George Gallaccio
Broadcast: 8 February 1987, BBC1 (100m)
Observations: This is based on the last Marple story that Christie wrote in 1971.

9. 4.50 from Paddington (1987)

Cast: Maurice Denham, Joanna David, John Hallam, David Horovitch, David Waller, Ian Brimble, Andrew Burt, Jill Meager, Mona Bruce
Crew: Director Martyn Friend, Teleplay TR Bowen, Producer George Gallaccio
Broadcast: 25 December 1987, BBC1 (110m)
Observations: The character of Elspeth McGillicuddy had been replaced by Marple herself in the 1962 film version of this story (*Murder She Said*) – but here she is restored to her rightful place in the action. Maurice Denham had played Inspector Japp in the so-called comedy film *The Alphabet Murders* (1966). The 1957 novel from which this adaptation was taken had featured Inspector Craddock – here he is replaced, almost unnoticeably, by Detective Inspector Slack.

10. A Caribbean Mystery (1989)

Cast: Frank Middlemass, Donald Pleasence, Barbara Barnes, Stephen Bent, Robert Swan, Sue Lloyd, Michael Feast, Sheila Ruskin, TP McKenna
Crew: Director Christopher Petit, Teleplay TR Bowen, Producer George Gallaccio.
Broadcast: 25 December 1989, BBC1 (100m)
Observations: Location filming in Barbados combined with the talents of Frank Middlemass, Donald Pleasence and TP McKenna make this dramatisation of Christie's 1964 novel a wonderful success.

11. They Do It with Mirrors (1991)

Cast: Jean Simmons, Joss Ackland, Faith Brook, John Bott, Gillian Barge, David Horovitch, Holly Aird, Todd Boyce, Christopher Villiers
Crew: Director Norman Stone, Teleplay TR Bowen, Producer Paul Gallaccio
Broadcast: 29 December 1991, BBC1 (100m)
Observations: After missing a year, it was good to have another Joan Hickson Marple story for Christmas, this time an adaptation of the 1952 story.

12. The Mirror Crack'd from Side to Side (1992)

Cast: Claire Bloom, Barry Newman, Elizabeth Garvie, Constantine Gregory, John Castle, David Horovitch, Glynis Barber, Amanda Elwes, Gwen Watford, Ian Brimble, Margaret Courtenay
Crew: Director Norman Stone, Teleplay TR Bowen, Producer Paul Gallaccio
Broadcast: 27 December 1992, BBC1 (115m)
Observations: Joan Hickson, then 86, appeared for the last time as Miss Jane Marple in this adaptation of the 1962 novel. Gwen Watford returned as her friend Dolly Bantry, a rôle she had played in the first BBC production back in 1985. Margaret Courtenay also appeared in the 1980 film version of *The Mirror Crack'd*.

Overall Verdict: Excellent, true-to-the-book adaptations. **5/5**

Geraldine McEwan as Miss Marple

Born in 1930 in Windsor, Geraldine McEwan was a leading British stage actress from the 1950s onwards, appearing in such productions as *Loot*, *The School for Scandal*, *The Browning Version* and *The Chairs*, for which she won a Tony Award for Best Actress in 1998. On television she could be seen in *The Barchester Chronicles* (1982), *Mapp and Lucia* (1985) and *Oranges Are Not the Only Fruit* (1990). She allegedly declined an OBE in 1986 and a DBE in 2002. She died on 30 January 2015 at the age of 82.

Agatha Christie's Marple (2004–2009)

1. The Body in the Library (2004)

Cast: Simon Callow, Jack Davenport, James Fox, Joanna Lumley, Jamie Theakston, Giles Oldershaw, Emma Cooke, Richard Durden, Adam Garcia, Florence Hoath, Ben Miller, Ian Richardson, Tina Martin, Bruce Mackinnon, Abigail Neale-Wilkinson, Anna Rawlings, Robin Soans, Mary Stockley, Zoe Thorne, Emma Williams, Steven Williams, David Walliams, Tara Fitzgerald
Crew: Director Andy Wilson, Teleplay Kevin Elyot
Broadcast: 12 December 2004, ITV1 (95m)
Observations: The first new Miss Marple adventure (under the title of *Agatha Christie's Marple*) since Joan Hickson's arguably definitive interpretation of the rôle, this was a loose adaptation of Christie's 1940 novel, coincidentally the same one that began Hickson's BBC series.

2. The Murder at the Vicarage (2004)

Cast: Stephen Tompkinson, Jane Asher, Jason Flemyng, Herbert Lom, Miriam Margolyes, Tim McInnerny, Janet McTeer, Robert Powell, Rachael Stirling, Mark Gatiss, Emily Bruni, Jana Carpenter, Christina Cole, Paul Hawkyard, Siobhan Hayes, Jenny Howe, Julian Morris, John Owens, Angela Pleasence, Ruth Sheen, Julie Cox, Marc Warren, Stephen Churchett
Crew: Director Charles Palmer, Teleplay Stephen Churchett
Broadcast: 19 December 2004, ITV1 (95m)
Observations: An adaptation of the first Miss Marple novel from 1930.

3. 4.50 from Paddington (2004)

Cast: Amanda Holden, Pam Ferris, John Hannah, Niamh Cusack, Celia Imrie, Griff Rhys-Jones, David Warner, Jenny Agutter, Rob Brydon, Tasha Bertham, Charlie Creed-Miles, Ben Daniels, Rose Keegan, Michael Landes, Martixell Lavanchy, Toby Marlow, Neve McIntosh, Ciarán McMenamin, Kurtis O'Brien, Tim Stern, Pip Torrens
Crew: Director Andy Wilson, Teleplay Stephen Churchett
Broadcast: 26 December 2004, ITV1 (95m)
Observations: A version of the 1957 novel with many extra elements.

4. A Murder is Announced (2005)

Cast: Zoë Wanamaker, Alexander Armstrong, Elaine Page, Virginia McKenna, Frances Barber, Cherie Lunghi, Christian Coulson, Richard Dickson, Matthew Goode, Sienna Guillory, Keeley Hawes, Gerald Horan, Nicole Lewis, Lesley Nicol, Christian Pederson, Robert Pugh, Claire Skinner, Catherine Tate
Crew: Director John Strickland, Teleplay Stewart Harcourt
Broadcast: 2 January 2005, ITV1 (95m)
Observations: Based on Christie's 1950 novel.

5. Sleeping Murder (2006)

Cast: Sophia Myles, Harriet Walter, Una Stubbs, Paul McGann, Sarah Parish, Martin Kemp, Dawn French, Phil Davis, Russ Abbot, Julian Wadham, Emilio Doorgasingh, Aidan McArdle, Harry Treadaway, Richard Bremmer, Anna-Louise Plowman, Greg Hicks, Mary Healey, Peter Serafinowicz, Helen Coker, Nickolas Grace, Geraldine Chaplin
Crew: Director John Hall, Teleplay Stephen Churchett
Broadcast: 5 February 2006, ITV1 (95m)
Observations: Loosely based on a novel Christie wrote in the 1940s detailing Miss Marple's last case; it was published posthumously in 1976.

6. The Moving Finger (2006)

Cast: James D'Arcy, Ken Russell, Frances de la Tour, Thelma Barlow, Jessica Hynes, Sean Pertwee, Kelly Brook, Harry Enfield, Imogen Stubbs, John Sessions, Rosalind Knight, Emilia Fox, Keith Allen, Ellen Capron, Talulah Riley, Angela Curran, Stephen Churchett
Crew: Director Tom Shankland, Teleplay Kevin Elyot
Broadcast: 12 February 2006, ITV1 (95m)
Observations: An unusually faithful adaptation of the 1942 novel.

7. By the Pricking of My Thumbs (2006)

Cast: Anthony Andrews, Greta Scacchi, June Whitfield, Claire Bloom, Steven Berkoff, Patrick Barlow, Josie Lawrence, Michelle Ryan, Charles Dance, Bonnie Langford, Brian Conley, Leslie Phillips, Chloe Pennington, Oliver Jordan, Clare Holman, Miriam Karlin, O-T Fagbenle, Jody Halse, Michael Maloney, Michael Begley, Lia Williams, Eliza Bennett, Florence Strickland

Crew: Director Peter Medak, Teleplay Stewart Harcourt
Broadcast: 19 February 2006, ITV1 (95m)
Observations: Based on the 1968 Tommy and Tuppence Beresford novel, with Tommy's role largely taken by Miss Marple.

8. The Sittaford Mystery (2006)

Cast: Timothy Dalton, Robert Hardy, Laurence Fox, Mel Smith, Rita Tushingham, Carey Mulligan, James Wilby, Paul Kaye, Michael Brandon, Patricia Hodge, Matthew Kelly, Robert Hickson, James Murray, Ian Hallard, Zoe Telford, Jeffery Kissoon, Michael Attwell
Crew: Director Paul Unwin, Teleplay Stephen Churchett
Broadcast: 30 April 2006, ITV1 (95m)
Observations: Miss Marple is successfully inserted into this supernaturally themed stand-alone 1931 novel.

9. At Bertram's Hotel (2007)

Cast: Martine McCutcheon, Mark Heap, Peter Davison, Danny Webb, Stephen Mangan, Francesca Annis, Isabella Parriss, James Howard, Adam Smethurst, Tony Bignell, Vincent Regan, Emily Beecham, Mary Nighy, Ed Stoppard, Charles Kay, Nicholas Burns, Mica Paris, Shenton Dixon, Polly Walker, Hannah Spearritt, Sarah London, Georgia Allen
Crew: Director Dan Zeff, Teleplay Tom MacRae
Broadcast: 23 September 2007, ITV1 (95m)
Observations: Based in the loosest way possible on the 1965 novel.

10. Ordeal by Innocence (2007)

Cast: Denis Lawson, Juliet Stevenson, Alison Steadman, Richard Armitage, Lisa Stansfield, Burn Gorman, Reece Shearsmith, Stephanie Leonidas, Jane Seymour, Tom Riley, Camille Coduri, Julian Rhind-Tutt, Bryan Dick, Gugu Mbatha-Raw, Andrea Lowe, Pippa Haywood, Michael Feast, James Hurran
Crew: Director Moira Armstrong, Teleplay Stewart Harcourt
Broadcast: 30 September 2007, ITV1 (95m)
Observations: The Marple-free 1958 novel acts as the starting point for this heavily altered adaptation.

11. Towards Zero (2008)

Cast: Paul Nicholls, Greg Wise, Tom Baker, Eileen Atkins, Alan Davies, Julian Sands, Zoë Tapper, Saffron Burrows, Julie Graham, Greg Rusedski, Wendy Nottingham, Amelda Brown, Peter Symonds, Eleanor Turner-Moss, Guy Williams, Jo Woodcock, Ben Meyjes, Thomas Arnold, Mike Burnside, Stewart Bewley
Crew: Directors David Grindley & Nicolas Winding Refn, Teleplay Kevin Elyot
Broadcast: 3 August 2008, ITV1 (95m)
Observations: Miss Marple is inserted into an otherwise largely faithful adaptation of the 1944 stand-alone novel.

12. Nemesis (2009)

Cast: Richard E Grant, Graeme Garden, Johnny Briggs, Ronni Ancona, Emily Woof, Anne Reid, Amanda Burton, Laura-Michelle Kelly, Dan Stevens, Ruth Wilson, Adrian Rawlins, Will Mellor, Lee Ingleby, Heidi Monsen
Crew: Director Nicolas Winding Refn, Teleplay Stephen Churchett
Broadcast: 1 January 2009, ITV1 (95m)
Observations: A typically fluid adaptation of Christie's final Miss Marple novel, published in 1971.

Overall Verdict: Geraldine McEwan puts in rather a mannered performance as the title character, and the eclectic guest cast – Greg Rusedski, Lisa Stansfield, Mel Smith for example – can sometimes prove distracting. Enjoyably bright and breezy, if more Light Entertainment than Drama. **3/5**

Julia McKenzie as Miss Marple

This popular character actress was born in Enfield, Middlesex in 1941 and has enjoyed a varied career in West End musicals, plays, sitcoms and films, mainly in light-hearted rôles. Prior to Miss Marple, she was best known for playing Anton Rodgers' wife in the Thames TV sitcom *Fresh Fields* (1984–86) and its sequel *French Fields* (1989–91). When Geraldine McEwan stepped down from the rôle in 2009, McKenzie took over as Miss Marple in a straightforward continuation of the series.

Agatha Christie's Marple (2009–2013)

1. A Pocket Full of Rye (2009)

Cast: Kenneth Cranham, Rupert Graves, Matthew Macfadyen, Ralf Little, Helen Baxendale, Ken Campbell, Wendy Richard, Edward Tudor-Pole, Prunella Scales, Rose Heiney, Laura Haddock, Thea Collings, Lucy Cohu, Anna Madeley, Joseph Beattie, Ben Miles, Liz White, Hattie Morahan, Paul Brooke, Chris Larkin
Crew: Director Charles Palmer, Teleplay Kevin Elyot
Broadcast: 6 September 2009, ITV1 (95m)
Observations: Julia McKenzie makes for a more sprightly, less mannered Marple in a pleasingly solid adaptation of the 1953 novel.

2. Murder is Easy (2009)

Cast: Jemma Redgrave, Russell Tovey, David Haig, Anna Chancellor, Hugo Speer, Tim Brooke-Taylor, Benedict Cumberbatch, Steve Pemberton, Shirley Henderson, Sylvia Sims, Lyndsey Marshal, James Lance, Camilla Arfwedson, Margo Stilley, Steven Hartley, Stephen Churchett
Crew: Director Hettie Macdonald, Teleplay Stephen Churchett
Broadcast: 13 September 2009, ITV1 (95m)
Observations: Miss Marple is inserted into this imaginative reworking of the stand-alone 1939 mystery.

3. They Do It With Mirrors (2010)

Cast: Joan Collins, Penelope Wilton, Brian Cox, Alexei Sayle, Ian Ogilvy, Sean Hughes, Elliot Cowan, Emma Griffiths Malin, Jordan Long, Sarah Smart, Maxine Peake, Liam Garrigan, Tom Payne, Nigel Terry, Alex Jennings
Crew: Director Andy Wilson, Teleplay Paul Rutman
Broadcast: 1 January 2010, ITV1 (95m)
Observations: A generally faithful adaptation of the 1952 novel.

4. The Pale Horse (2010)

Cast: Jonathan Cake, Nigel Planer, Lynda Baron, Nicholas Parsons, Pauline Collins, Holly Valance, Bill Paterson, Neil Pearson, JJ Feild, Jodie Hay, Jason Merrells, Jenny Galloway, Susan Lynch, Tom Ward, Sarah Alexander, Amy Manson, Mike Shepherd, Holly Willoughby, Julia Molony

Crew: Director Andy Hay, Teleplay Russell Lewis
Broadcast: 30 August 2010, ITV1 (95m)
Observations: An adaptation of the 1961 occult mystery, with Ariadne Oliver replaced by Miss Marple.

5. The Secret of Chimneys (2010)

Cast: Edward Fox, Jonas Armstrong, Dervla Kirwan, Ruth Jones, Ian Weichardt, Laura O'Toole, Robert Dunbar, Mathew Horne, Adam Godley, Charlotte Salt, Michelle Collins, Anthony Higgins, Alex Knight, Stephen Dillane, Letty Butler, Nicci Brighten
Crew: Director John Strickland, Teleplay Paul Rutman
Broadcast: 27 December 2010, ITV1 (95m)
Observations: Many changes were made to the original 1925 stand-alone novel, not the least of which is the insertion of Miss Marple.

6. The Blue Geranium (2010)

Cast: Toby Stephens, Kevin McNally, Donald Sinden, Claire Rushbrook, David Calder, Paul Rhys, Sharon Small, Claudia Blakley, Joanna Page, Ian East, Derek Hutchinson, Jason Durr, Patrick Baladi, Caroline Catz, Rebekah Manning, Hugh Ross
Crew: Director David Moore, Teleplay Stewart Harcourt
Broadcast: 29 December 2010, ITV1 (95m)
Observations: Based on a short story in *The Thirteen Problems* (1932).

7. The Mirror Crack'd from Side to Side (2011)

Cast: Lindsay Duncan, Joanna Lumley, Caroline Quentin, Martin Jarvis, Michele Dotrice, Hugh Bonneville, Gene Goodman, Isabella Parriss, Jonny Coyne, Nigel Harman, Victoria Smurfit, Brennan Brown, Hannah Waddingham, Olivia Darnley, Charlotte Riley, Don Gallagher, Lois Jones, Neil Stuke, Samuel Barnett, Will Young, Anna Anderson
Crew: Director Tom Shankland, Teleplay Kevin Elyot
Broadcast: 2 January 2011, ITV1 (95m)
Observations: Based on the 1962 novel.

8. Why Didn't They Ask Evans? (2011)

Cast: Helen Lederer, Georgia Moffett, Samantha Bond, Richard Briers, Rik Mayall, Rafe Spall, Warren Clarke, Mark Williams, Sean Biggerstaff,

David Buchanan, Siwan Morris, Freddie Fox, Hannah Murray, Natalie Dormer
Crew: Director Nicholas Renton, Teleplay Patrick Barlow
Broadcast: 15 June 2011, ITV1 (95m)
Observations: A reworked version of the Marple-free 1934 novel.

9. A Caribbean Mystery (2013)

Cast: Robert Webb, Hermione Norris, Anthony Sher, Pippa Bennett Warner, Charity Wakefield, Warren Brown, Alastair Mackenzie, Charles Mesure, MyAnna Buring, Kingsley Ben-Adir, Montserrat Lombard, Oliver Ford Davies, Daniel Rigby, Andrea Dondolo, Joe Vaz, Anele Matoti, Jeremy Crutchley, Charlie Higson
Crew: Director Charles Palmer, Teleplay Charlie Higson
Broadcast: 16 June 2013, ITV (95m)
Observations: Colourful adaptation of the 1964 novel, with some sly 007 in-jokes.

10. Greenshaw's Folly (2013)

Cast: Julia Sawalha, Robert Glenister, Fiona Shaw, John Gordon Sinclair, Rufus Jones, Vic Reeves, Kimberley Nixon, Bobby Smalldridge, Martin Compston, Sam Reid, Joanna David, Judy Parfitt, Candida Gubbins, Matt Willis, Oscar Pearce
Crew: Director Sarah Harding, Teleplay Tim Whitnall
Broadcast: 23 June 2013, ITV (95m)
Observations: Based on two short stories: 'Greenshaw's Folly' from *The Adventure of the Christmas Pudding and a Selection of Entrées* (1960) and 'The Thumb Mark of St Peter' from *The Thirteen Problems* (1932).

11. Endless Night (2013)

Cast: Wendy Craig, Tamzin Outhwaite, Glynis Barber, Hugh Dennis, Tom Hughes, Aneurin Barnard, Adam Wadsworth, Joanna Vanderham, Janet Henfrey, William Hope, Michael McKell, Birgitte Hjort Sørensen, Rosalind Halstead, Celyn Jones, Stephen Churchett
Crew: Director David Moore, Teleplay Kevin Elyot
Broadcast: 29 December 2013, ITV (95m)
Observations: Miss Marple is added to the original 1967 novel.

Overall Verdict: Julia McKenzie brings some gentle refinement to the part, while the plotting settles down a little and the stories overall appear rather less silly. Quirky casting aside (Holly Willoughby, Will Young), the series concludes on a positive note. **4/5**

Miscellaneous Television

All colour UK productions unless otherwise specified.

1. Ten Little Niggers (1949)

Cast: Bruce Belfrage, John Stuart, John Bentley, Arthur Wontner, Campbell Singer, Sally Rogers, Margery Bryce, Douglas Hurn, Stanley Lemin, Elizabeth Maude, Barry Steele
Crew: Directed & Produced by Kevin Sheldon, Writer Kevin Sheldon (based on Agatha Christie's stage play)
Broadcast: 20 August 1949, b/w, BBC (90m)
Observations: For Christie's first TV outing, theatre director Kevin Sheldon elected to use her original play script for this live performance. Wontner had played Sherlock Holmes in five British films of the 1930s, John Bentley was the hero of many a low-budget adventure film (such as *Calling Paul Temple*, 1948) and Bruce Belfrage was well known as a leading BBC newsreader of the 1940s. The adaptation was faithful to the stage play, using the theatrical version of the ending, rather than the one Christie had used for her 1939 book.
Verdict: Fluffs aside, a pretty good adaptation. **4/5**

2. A Murder is Announced (1956)

Cast: Gracie Fields, Jessica Tandy, Roger Moore, Betty Sinclair, Josephine Brown, Pat Nye, Malcolm Kuin
Crew: Director Delbert Mann, Teleplay Louis S Peterson, Producer Fred Coe
US Broadcast: 30 December 1956, b/w, NBC (55m)
Observations: Presented as part of the Goodyear TV Playhouse series, the British stage and music hall singer Gracie Fields portrayed Miss Marple for the first time in any medium in this dramatisation of the 1950 novel.
Verdict: Odd casting, but a reasonably faithful rendition of the book. **3/5**

3. Ten Little Niggers (1959)

Cast: Viola Keats, Harry Locke, Norman Mitchell, Christine Pollon, John Stone, Michael Scott, Wensley Pithey, Laidman Browne, Mary Hinton, Felix Aylmer, John Gabriel
Crew: Director and Teleplay Robert Tronson
Broadcast: 13 January 1959, b/w, ITV (90m, Associated Rediffusion)
Observations: Little-known adaptation, eclipsed by the version a decade earlier.
Verdict: A strong cast of dependable character actors make this version well worth a look. **4/5**

4. The Seven Dials Mystery (1981)

Cast: Sir John Gielgud, Harry Andrews, Terence Alexander, Cheryl Campbell, James Warwick, Lucy Gutteridge, Rula Lenska, Leslie Sands, Christopher Scoular, Brian Wilde, Roger Sloman
Crew: Director Tony Wharmby, Adapted by Pat Sandys, Producer Jack Williams
Broadcast: 8 March 1981, ITV (131m, LWT)
Observations: Based on the 1929 novel, this adaptation was filmed at Christie's own home, Greenway House in Devon. James Warwick would go on to star as Tommy Beresford in the 1984 LWT series *Partners in Crime*.
Verdict: Excellent period detail, if rather slow. **3/5**

5. Why Didn't They Ask Evans? (1981)

Cast: Sir John Gielgud, Lord Bernard Miles, Francesca Annis, James Warwick, Leigh Lawson, Connie Booth, Eric Porter, James Cossins, Madeleine Smith, Robert Longden, Joan Hickson, Norman Mitchell
Crew: Directors John Davies & Tony Wharmby, Teleplay Pat Sandys, Producer Jack Williams
Broadcast: 30 March 1981, ITV (169m, LWT)
Observations: The same team who made *The Seven Dials Mystery* produced this adaptation of Christie's 1934 comedy thriller. Francesca Annis would go on to co-star in 1984's *Partners in Crime* while Joan Hickson, who had already appeared in three other Christie adaptations, would later star as the definitive Miss Marple for the BBC.
Verdict: An entertaining adaptation, although its resolution confused many. **4/5**

6. Murder Is Easy (1982)

Cast: Bill Bixby, Lesley Ann Down, Olivia De Havilland, Timothy West, Helen Hayes, Freddie Jones, Patrick Allen, Leigh Lawson, Shane Briant, Anthony Valentine, Jonathan Pryce
Crew: Director Claude Whatham, Teleplay Carmen Culver, Producers David L Wolper & Stan Margulies
US Broadcast: 2 January 1982, CBS (97m, Warner Bros)
Observations: Made by the producers of the TV series *Roots*, this was a faithful adaptation of the 1939 novel (apart from the absence of Superintendent Battle) which featured an almost solely English cast on location in England. Future Miss Marple Helen Hayes appears in a small rôle.
Verdict: A workmanlike production, a bit soft around the edges. **3/5**

7. Witness for the Prosecution (1982)

Cast: Sir Ralph Richardson, Diana Rigg, Deborah Kerr, Beau Bridges, Dame Wendy Hiller, Donald Pleasence, David Langton, Richard Vernon, Michael Gough, Peter Sallis, Peter Copley, Aubrey Woods
Crew: Director Alan Gibson, Teleplay John Gay, Producer Norman Rosemont
US Broadcast: 4 December 1982, CBS (101m, United Artists)
Observations: The screenplay was based on the 1953 stage play, as well as the 1957 Billy Wilder film version. Although the American actor Beau Bridges was cast as Leonard Vole, in Christie's original 1933 short story the character is British.
Verdict: Hard to see the point of this when the film does it so much better, but good to see Richardson giving his all. **3/5**

8. The Agatha Christie Hour (1982)

This ten-part Thames Television series was produced by Pat Sandys, with John Frankau as executive producer. There is no link between the short story adaptations, two of which contain the only appearances to date of Mr Parker Pyne.

1) The Case of the Middle-Aged Wife
Cast: Maurice Denham, Gwen Watford, Michael Simpson, Peter Jones, Kate Dorning
Crew: Director Michael Simpson, Teleplay Freda Kelsall

Broadcast: 7 September 1982, ITV (55m)
Observations: Taken from *Parker Pyne Investigates* (1934).

2) In a Glass Darkly

Cast: Nicholas Clay, Emma Piper, Johnathon Morris, Elspeth Gray
Crew: Director Desmond Davis, Teleplay William Corlett
Broadcast: 14 September 1982, ITV (55m)
Observations: Taken from *The Regatta Mystery* (1939*).

3) The Girl in the Train

Cast: Osmond Bullock, Sarah Berger, Ron Pember, James Grout, Roy Kinnear, Bill Treacher
Crew: Director Brian Farnham, Teleplay William Corlett
Broadcast: 21 September 1982, ITV (55m)
Observations: Taken from *The Listerdale Mystery* (1934†).

4) The Fourth Man

Cast: John Nettles, Prue Clark, Michael Gough, Roy Leighton, Frederick Jaeger, Fiona Mathieson
Crew: Director Michael Simpson, Teleplay William Corlett
Broadcast: 28 September 1982, ITV (55m)
Observations: Taken from *The Hound of Death* (1933†).

5) The Case of the Discontented Soldier

Cast: Maurice Denham, Lally Bowers, William Gaunt, Patricia Garwood, Lewis Fiander
Crew: Director Michael Simpson, Teleplay TR Bowen
Broadcast: 5 October 1982, ITV (55m)
Observation: Taken from *Parker Pyne Investigates* (1934).

6) Magnolia Blossom

Cast: Ralph Bates, Ciaran Madden, Jeremy Clyde, Alexandra Basted, Brian Oulton, Jack May
Crew: Director John Frankau, Teleplay John Bryden Rodgers
Broadcast: 12 October 1982, ITV (55m)
Observation: Taken from *The Golden Ball* (1971*).

7) The Mystery of the Blue Jar

Cast: Michael Aldridge, Robin Kermode, Isabelle Spade, Derek Francis, Hugh Walters
Crew: Director Cyril Coke, Teleplay TR Bowen

Broadcast: 19 October 1982, ITV (55m)
Observation: Taken from *The Hound of Death* (1933†).

8) The Red Signal
Cast: Christopher Cazenove, Joanna David, Richard Morant, Carol Drinkwater, Michael Denison
Crew: Director John Frankau, Teleplay William Corlett
Broadcast: 2 November 1982, ITV (55m)
Observation: Taken from *The Hound of Death* (1933†).

9) Jane in Search of a Job
Cast: Amanda Redman, Elizabeth Garvie, Andrew Bicknell, Tony Jay, Stephanie Cole, Geoffrey Hinsliff
Crew: Director Christopher Hodson, Teleplay Gerald Savory
Broadcast: 9 November 1982, ITV (55m)
Observation: Taken from *The Listerdale Mystery* (1934†).

10) The Manhood of Edward Robinson
Cast: Nicholas Farrell, Cherie Lunghi, Ann Thornton, Patrick Newell
Crew: Director Brian Farnham, Teleplay Gerald Savory
Broadcast: 16 November 1982, ITV (55m)
Observation: Taken from *The Listerdale Mystery* (1934†).

Overall Verdict: A cracking good series, rather like a period *Tales of the Unexpected*. **5/5**

9. Magnolia Blossom (1982)

Cast: Ralph Bates, Ciaran Madden, Jeremy Clyde
Crew: Director John Frankau, Teleplay John Bryden Rodgers, Producer Pat Sandys
Broadcast: 12 October 1982, ITV (50m, Thames TV)
Observation: Based on the short story from *The Golden Ball* (1971*).
Verdict: A strong cast heads a well-written adaptation of this lesser known story. **4/5**

10. Spider's Web (1982)

Cast: Penelope Keith, Robert Flemyng, Thorley Walters, Elisabeth Spriggs, David Yelland
Crew: Director Basil Coleman, Producer Cedric Messina
Broadcast: December 1982, BBC2 (90m, BBC)

Observations: This is an adaptation of Christie's 1954 stage play.
Verdict: Decent production values and a good cast. **4/5**

11. Sparkling Cyanide (1983)

Cast: Anthony Andrews, Harry Morgan, Deborah Raffin, Nancy Marchand, Barrie Ingham, Pamela Bellwood
Crew: Director Robert M Lewis, Teleplay Sue Grafton, Steve Humphrey & Robert M Young, Producer Stan Marguiles
US Broadcast: 5 November 1983, CBS (94m, Warner Bros TV)
Observations: Christie's 1945 novel was updated to 1980s Los Angeles.
Verdict: Change of location aside, this is a reasonable stab at a tricky story. **3/5**

12. The Secret Adversary (1983)

Cast: James Warwick (Tommy), Francesca Annis (Tuppence), Reece Dinsdale, Peter Barkworth, Alec McCowen, George Baker, Honor Blackman, John Fraser, Donald Houston
Crew: Director Tony Wharmby, Teleplay Pat Sandys, Producer Jack Williams
Broadcast: 9 October 1983, ITV (107m, LWT)
Observations: Half a century after Christie's 1922 novel was first filmed (as *Adventure Ltd*), it received its first television outing.
Verdict: A splendid all-star adaptation, this acted as the perfect introduction to the series that followed. **5/5**

13. Partners in Crime (1983)

Cast: James Warwick (Tommy), Francesca Annis (Tuppence), Reece Dinsdale (Albert)

1) The Affair of the Pink Pearl
Cast: Graham Crowden, Arthur Cox, Dulcie Gray, Noel Dyson, William Hootkins
Crew: Director Tony Wharmby, Teleplay David Butler
Broadcast: 16 October 1983, ITV (52m)

2) The House of Lurking Death
Cast: Joan Sanderson, Liz Smith, Lynsey Baxter, Michael Cochrane, Anita Dobson

Crew: Director Christopher Hodson, Teleplay Jonathan Hales
Broadcast: 23 October 1983, ITV (52m)

3) Finessing the King
Cast: Benjamin Whitrow, Annie Lambert, Arthur Cox, Peter Blythe
Crew: Director Christopher Hodson, Teleplay Gerald Savory
Broadcast: 30 October 1983, ITV (52m)

4) The Clergyman's Daughter
Cast: Geoffrey Drew, Bill Dean, Elspeth MacNaughton, Pam St Clement, Alan Jones
Crew: Directer & Teleplay Paul Annett
Broadcast: 6 November 1983, ITV (52m)

5) The Sunningdale Mystery
Cast: Edwin Brown, Emily Moore, Denis Holmes, Terence Conoley
Crew: Director Tony Wharmby, Teleplay Jonathan Hales
Broadcast: 13 November 1983, ITV (52m)

6) The Ambassador's Boots
Cast: TP McKenna, Jennie Linden, Arthur Cox, Clive Merrison, Catherine Schell
Crew: Director & Teleplay Paul Annett
Broadcast: 20 November 1983, ITV (52m)

7) The Man in the Mist
Cast: Linda Marlowe, Tim Brierley, Anne Stallybrass, Constantine Gregory
Crew: Director Christopher Hodson, Teleplay Gerald Savory
Broadcast: 27 November 1983, ITV (52m)

8) The Case of the Missing Lady
Cast: Jonathan Newth, Rowena Cooper, Ewan Hooper, Elizabeth Murray
Crew: Director & Teleplay Paul Annatt
Broadcast: 4 December 1983, ITV (52m)

9) The Unbreakable Alibi
Cast: Tim Meats, Anna Nygh, Michael Jayes, Ellis Dale
Crew: Director Christopher Hodson, Teleplay David Butler
Broadcast: 11 December 1983, ITV (52m)

10) *The Crackler*
Cast: Shane Rimmer, Arthur Cox, Christopher Scoular, Carole Rosseau
Crew: Director Christopher Hodson, Teleplay Gerald Savory
Broadcast: 18 December 1983, ITV (52m)

Overall Observations: This popular LWT series presented ten of the fifteen short stories found in the 1929 short story collection. It was produced by Jack Williams at a cost of £2m.
Overall Verdict: Highly enjoyable and well cast. **5/5**

14. Murder by the Book (1986)

Cast: Dame Peggy Ashcroft (Christie), Ian Holm (Poirot), Richard Wilson, Michael Aldridge, Dawn Archibald
Crew: Director Lawrence Gordon Clark, Teleplay Nick Evans, Producers Nick Evans & Dickie Bamber
Broadcast: 28 August 1986, ITV (52m, TVS)
Observations: This unusual drama has Poirot appearing to Agatha Christie in a dream and accusing her of killing him off.
Verdict: Appealing in a loopy kind of way. **3/5**

15. The Last Séance (1986)

Cast: Jeanne Moreau, Anthony Higgins, Norma West
Crew: Director & Producer June Wyndham-Davies, Teleplay Alfred Shaughnessy
Broadcast: 27 September 1986, ITV (50m, Granada)
Observations: An adaptation of a short story from the 1933 collection *The Hound of Death*, this was the final part in a supernatural anthology series entitled *Shades of Darkness*.
Verdict: A somewhat muted production, the last in a generally excellent series. **3/5**

16. The Man in the Brown Suit (1989)

Cast: Stephanie Zimbalist, Rue McClanahan, Tony Randall, Edward Woodward, Ken Howard, Nickolas Grace, Simon Duttin
Crew: Director Alan Grint, Teleplay Carla Jean Wagner, Producer Alan Shayne
US Broadcast: 4 January 1989 (90m, Warner Bros TV)
Observations: Based on the 1924 novel, the action shifts from England to Cairo, but was actually filmed in Madrid and Cadiz.
Verdict: A distinctly below-average adaptation – the actors appear to have been chosen for their appeal to American viewers rather than their suitability. **2/5**

17. The Pale Horse (1997)

Cast: Colin Buchanan, Jayne Ashbourne, Hermione Norris, Leslie Phillips, Michael Byrne, Geoffrey Beevers, Louise Jameson, Ruth Madoc, Jean Marsh, Richard O'Callaghan, Andy Serkis
Crew: Director Charles Beeson, Teleplay Alma Cullen, Producers Guy Slater & Adrian Bate
Broadcast: 23 December 1997, ITV (101m, A&E Television)
Observations: An American production with a strong English cast (including future Gollum actor Andy Serkis), this was a loosely adapted TV movie taken from the 1961 supernatural novel.
Verdict: A surprisingly atmospheric little chiller with some excellent performances. **5/5**

18. Murder on the Orient Express (2001)

Cast: Alfred Molina (Poirot), Meredith Baxter, Leslie Caron, Anira Casar, Nicolas Chagrin, Tasha De Vasconcelos, David Hunt, Adam James, Peter Strauss
Crew: Director Carl Schenkel, Teleplay Stephen Harrigan, Producer Marion Rosenberg
US Broadcast: 22 April 2001, CBS (89m, Daniel H Blatt Productions)
Observations: Based on the 1934 classic novel, this was the first independent Christie adaptation for over a decade.
Verdict: An updated version of a much-loved story done without much enthusiasm for the subject matter. **2/5**

19. Sparkling Cyanide (2003)

Cast: Pauline Collins, Oliver Ford Davies, Kenneth Cranham, Jonathan Firth, Susan Hampshire, Clare Holman, James Wilby, Lia Williams, Dominic Cooper
Crew: Director Tristram Powell, Teleplay Laura Lamson
Broadcast: 5 October 2003, ITV1 (100m, Thames)
Observations: An updated version of the 1945 novel.
Verdict: A surprisingly enjoyable modernised retelling of a fairly standard Christie whodunit. **4/5**

20. Partners in Crime (2015)

Cast: David Walliams (Tommy), Jessica Raine (Tuppence), Matthew Steer (Albert)

1) The Secret Adversary
Crew: Director Edward Hall, Teleplay Zinnie Harris
Broadcast: 2015, BBC1

2) N or M?
Crew: Director Edward Hall, Teleplay Claire Wilson
Broadcast: 2015, BBC1

21

Original Fiction

Books

The Monogram Murders (HarperCollins, 2014)

Author: Sophie Hannah

Case: Hercule Poirot investigates a series of fiendish murders in a top London hotel...

Context: British crime writer and poet Sophie Hannah was selected by Christie's grandson Mathew Prichard to write a new novel featuring Hercule Poirot as a prelude to the author's 125th anniversary in 2015.

Conclusion: A cleverly plotted mystery story, set in a convincing locale, even though the character of Poirot bears only a passing resemble to Christie's inimitable original. **4/5**

22
Reference Materials

Books

The Agatha Christie Who's Who by Randall Toye (Holt Rinehart & Winston, 1980). A good reference book to all the main Christie characters.

Agatha Christie: The Art of Her Crimes [commentary] by Julian Symons (Everest House, 1981). Beautiful selection of Tom Adams' iconic 1970s paperback cover art.

Agatha Christie's Crossword Puzzle Book by Randall Toye (Henry Holt, 1981). Crosswords, Christie – what more is there to say?

Agatha Christie: A Biography by Janet Morgan (HarperCollins, 1984). A well written life story that neatly counterpoints Christie's own selective memoirs.

The Agatha Christie Companion by Dennis Sanders and Len Lovallo (WH Allen, 1985). A guide to the whole Christie phenomenon, crammed full of information, with synopses, character lists, contemporary reviews and first edition details for every story. Appendices cover major characters' appearances and there is a potted Christie biography and timeline. Highly recommended.

Agatha Christie's Poirot: The Life and Times of Hercules Poirot by Anne Hart (Pavilion, 1990). Handsomely presented character study of Belgium's most famous detective, with extracts from the novels, a run-down of film and television appearances and a comprehensive bibliography.

Murder in Four Acts by Peter Haining (Virgin, 1990) Centenary celebration of the 'Queen of Crime' on stage, film, radio and television.

Agatha Christie: The Woman and Her Mysteries by Gillian Gill (Free Press, 1990). Feminist interpretation of Christie's life and an intriguing view of some of her most famous characters.

The Films of Agatha Christie by Scott Palmer (Batsford, 1993). Worth getting for the photographs, but the written content is lacking critical analysis and as it's from an American perspective, transmission dates are misleading. The title is a misnomer – television adaptations are also covered.

Agatha Christie's Marple: The Life and Times of Miss Jane Marple by Anne Hart (HarperCollins, 1997). A slim but beautifully presented volume detailing every fact you could possibly want to know about this eminent elderly sleuth.

Agatha Christie and the Eleven Missing Days by Jared Cade (Peter Owen, 1998). An exhaustively researched investigation of Christie's famous disappearance.

The Life and Crimes of Agatha Christie by Charles Osborne (HarperCollins, 1999). This covers all the books and adaptations, although not being primarily a 'list book' the information is harder to access. But what it lacks in detail it more than makes up for in analysis and informed opinion.

The World of Agatha Christie by Martin Fido (Carlton, 1999). Of more interest for the visual material than the written stuff, which is fairly anodyne.

The Bedside, Bathtub and Armchair Companion to Agatha Christie by Dick Riley and Pam McAllister (Continuum, 2001). A veritable brick of a book, with maps, puzzles, photos, film posters and spoiler-free synopses of every Christie novel and short story.

Agatha Christie: The Finished Portrait by Dr Andrew Norman (History Press, 2006). The author's 11–day disappearance is put under the microscope by a former GP.

Agatha Christie's Secret Notebooks: Fifty Years of Mysteries in the Making by John Curran (HarperCollins, 2009). Fascinating titbits from the author's personal notebooks, including two unpublished short stories.

Agatha Christie's Murder in the Making: Stories and Secrets from Her Archive by John Curran (HarperCollins, 2011). More fascinating extracts from Christie's private notebooks, including a couple of 'new' stories, later rewritten.

The Agatha Christie Triviography and Quiz Book by Kathleen Kaska (LL-Publications, 2012). Sixty quizzes, 1001 questions, previously published in 1996 as *What's Your Agatha Christie IQ?*

The Grand Tour: Letters and Photographs from the British Empire Exhibition edited by Mathew Prichard (HarperCollins, 2013). A wealth of previously unpublished material from the author's extensive ten-month trade mission in 1922.

Poirot and Me by David Suchet (Headline, 2013). Fascinating insight into this busy actor's career during his quarter century of playing Poirot on television.

The Agatha Christie Miscellany by Cathy Cook (History Press, 2013). Slight but surprisingly readable assortment of trivia; ideal pub quiz source material.

Internet

Agatha Christie (www.agathachristie.com). The author's official home on the web, this site is jointly run by Acorn Productions Ltd and the Christie Archive Trust.

Agatha Christie – The Icelandic Homepage (www.isholf.is/jonasson/agatha). Not the first country you'd associate with Christie, but this is a very nice site with plenty of information.

Delicious Death: The Agatha Christie Works List (www.deliciousdeath.com). As much detail as you could possibly want on all of Christie's books, as well as film, TV and play adaptations. The site boasts reproductions of almost every book jacket – impressive.

Murder One (www.murderone.co.uk). Based on Charing Cross Road, this is the largest specialist crime bookstore in London (and the owner Maxim Jakubowski writes the odd crime book himself) – you can order Christie titles online here too.

Agatha Christie's Riviera (www.englishriviera.co.uk/agathachristie). This official online guide to the English Riviera offers a plethora of Christie-themed locations and activities, centring around her native birthplace of Torquay.

The International Agatha Christie Festival (www.agathachristiefestival.com). Official website for the now famous crime writing literary festival held annually since 2004.

Greenway House (www.nationaltrust.org.uk/greenway). Visitor information about Christie's beautiful house and gardens overlooking the river Dart, which opened to the public in 2009.

Poirot Central (www.poirot.us/poirot.php) Nicely presented site about the Belgian detective, which also covers Marple and other works.

Hercule Poirot (www.freewebs.com/poirot). Another fan-made site, this time with a short but intriguing essay comparing Poirot with Holmes.

Contact the author: If you would like to correspond with Mark Campbell and give him some feedback on this Pocket Essential, you can send an email to mark.campbell10@virgin.net.

Index